PENGUIN MODERN CLASSICS

FRUITS OF THE EARTH

André Paul Guillaume Gide was born in Paris on 22 November 1869. His father, who died when he was eleven, was Professor of Law at the Sorbonne. An only child, Gide had an irregular and lonely upbringing and was educated in a Protestant secondary school in Paris and privately. He became devoted to literature and music, and began his literary career as an essayist, and then went on to poetry, biography, fiction, drama, criticism, reminiscence, and translation. By 1917 he had emerged as a prophet to French youth and his unorthodox views were a source of endless debate and attack. In 1947 he was awarded the Nobel Prize for Literature and in 1948, as a distinguished foreigner, was given an honorary degree at Oxford. He married his cousin in 1892; he died in Paris in 1951 at the age of eighty-one. Gide's best-known works in England are *Strait is the Gate* (*La Porte étroite*), the first novel he wrote, which was published in France in 1909; *The Counterfeiters* (*Les Faux-Monnayeurs*) published in 1926; and the famous *Journals* covering his life from 1889 to 1949 and published originally in four volumes. These books, together with *The Immoralist, The Vatican Cellars, La Symphonie Pastorale* and *Isabelle* are all available in the Penguin Modern Classics.

ANDRÉ GIDE

Fruits of the Earth

PENGUIN BOOKS

in association with Secker & Warburg

Penguin Books Ltd, Harmondsworth, Middlesex, England
Penguin Books Inc., 7110 Ambassador Road, Baltimore, Maryland 21207, U.S.A.
Penguin Books Australia Ltd, Ringwood, Victoria, Australia
Penguin Books Canada Ltd, 41 Steelcase Road West, Markham, Ontario, Canada
Penguin Books (N.Z.) Ltd, 182–190 Wairau Road, Auckland 10, New Zealand

—

This translation first published by Martin Secker & Warburg 1949
Published in Penguin Modern Classics 1970
Reprinted 1972, 1976

—

Made and printed in Great Britain by
Hazell Watson & Viney Ltd,
Aylesbury, Bucks
Set in Monotype Garamond

'Food not of angels ...'
MILTON, *Paradise Lost*, Bk v, 465

Contents

FRUITS OF THE EARTH

Preface to the French Edition of 1927

July 1926

To this manual of escape, of liberation, it is customary to con-
fine me. The present reprint gives me the opportunity of
putting before my new readers a few reflections which, by
more precisely defining the motives and circumstances which
gave rise to it will tend to diminish its import.

1. *Fruits of the Earth* is the work of a man who, if not
actually ill, was recovering, or had recently recovered, from
illness – of a man, at any rate, who had been ill. In the very
flights of its poetry there is the exuberance of someone to
whom life is precious because he has been on the point of
losing it.

2. I wrote this book at a time when our literature was
terribly imbued with a close and artificial atmosphere, and it
seemed to me urgent that it should be brought down to earth
once more and step again with bare feet simply on the common
ground.

The book's lack of success shows how far it was at variance
with the taste of the day. Not a single critic mentioned it. In
the course of ten years barely five hundred copies were sold.

3. I wrote this book at a moment when I had just settled my
life; at a moment when I had voluntarily surrendered a liberty
which my book – a work of art – immediately laid claim to
with all the greater resolution. And in writing it I was, need-
less to say, perfectly sincere; but equally sincere in my heart's
epudiation of it.

4. Let me add that I had no intention of stopping short at
this book. I set down in it the features of the fluctuating and
disengaged state I was painting much as a novelist might
draw the characteristics of a hero who resembles himself but
who is his invention; and it seems to me to-day that I did not
draw them without detaching them, so to speak, from myself –
or, if you prefer it, without detaching myself from them.

5. I am usually judged by this book of my youth as if the ethics of *Fruits of the Earth* were the ethics of my whole life, as if I myself had not been the first to follow the advice I give my young reader: 'Throw away my book and leave me.' Yes, I immediately left the man I was when I wrote *Fruits of the Earth*; so much so that if I examine my life, the dominating feature I note in it, so far from being inconstancy, is, on the contrary, fidelity.

6. One word more. Some people can only see in this book – *will* only see in it – a glorification of desire and instinct. This seems to me a little short-sighted. As for me, when I reopen it, what strikes me even more is the apology I find in it of a life stripped to bareness. This is what I have retained, letting go the rest, and it is precisely to this that I still remain faithful. And it is to this I owe, as I mean some day to say, my subsequent adherence to the doctrine of the Gospels, finding in self-denial the most perfect self-realization, the highest exaction and the most boundless permission of happiness.

'May my book teach you to care more for yourself than for it, and then more for all the rest than for yourself.' This is what I said before in the Introduction to *Fruits of the Earth* and in its last lines. Why force me to repeat it?

Do not be deceived, Nathaniel, by the uncompromising title I have thought fit to give this book. I might have called it Menalcas; but Menalcas has never, any more than yourself, existed. The only man's name which might have been set to it is my own; but then how should I have dared sign it? I have put myself into it without affectation or shame; and if sometimes I speak in it of lands I have never visited, of perfumes I have never breathed, of actions I have never committed – or of you, my Nathaniel, whom I have not yet seen – it is not hypocrisy on my part, and these things are no more false than is this name I call you by, not knowing what yours will be – yours, Nathaniel, who will one day read me.

And when you have read me, throw this book away – and go out. May it have given you the desire to go out – to go out from wherever you may be, from your town, from your family, from your room, from your thoughts. Do not take my book with you. If I had been Menalcas, I should have led you by your right hand, but your left would not have known it, and soon – as soon as we were far from any town – I should have let go the hand I held and told you to forget me.

May my book teach you to care more for yourself than for it – and then more for all the rest than for yourself.

BOOK I

My idle happiness that slept so long
Is now at length awaking.
Hafiz

I

Do not try, Nathaniel, to find God *here* or *there* – but every-where.

Every creature points to God, none reveals Him.

Every creature we let our eyes dwell on distracts us from God.

While other people were publishing or working, I, on the contrary, devoted three years of travel to forgetting all that I had learnt with my head. This unlearning was slow and difficult; it was of more use to me than all the learning imposed by men, and was really the beginning of an education.

You will never know the efforts it cost us to become interested in life; but now that life does interest us, it will be, like everything else, passionately.

I chastised my flesh gladly, taking more pleasure in the chastisement than in the fault – so intoxicating was the pride I took in not sinning simply.

Suppress in yourself the idea of *merit* – one of the mind's greatest stumbling blocks.

. . . All our life long we have been tormented by the uncertainty of our paths. How can I put it? All choice, when one comes to think of it, is terrifying; liberty, when there is no duty to guide it, terrifying. The path that has to be chosen lies through a wholly unexplored country, where each one makes his own discoveries, and – note this – for himself alone; so that the vaguest track in the darkest Africa is more easily distinguishable. . . . Shady groves allure us and the mirage of perennial springs. Or rather, springs will flow where our desires bid them; for the country only comes into existence as our approach gives it form, and the landscape about us gradually falls into shape as we advance; we cannot see as far as the horizon; and even the foreground is nothing but a successive and changeable appearance.

17

But why comparisons when the matter is so serious? We all believe we shall eventually discover God. In the meantime, alas, where are we to address our prayers? At last we end by saying that He – the Unfindable – is everywhere, anywhere, and kneel down at haphazard.

And so, Nathaniel, you are like the man who should follow as his guide the light he holds in his own hand.

Wherever you go, you will never meet with anything but God. 'God,' said Menalcas, 'is what lies ahead of us.'

Nathaniel, look at everything as you pass on your way, but stay nowhere. Remember that it is only God who is not transitory.

Let the *importance* lie in your look, not in the thing you look at.

All your gathered knowledge of what is *outside* you will remain outside you to all eternity. Why do you attach so much importance to it?

There is profit in desires, and profit in the satisfaction of desires – for so they are increased. And indeed, Nathaniel, each one of my desires has enriched me more than the always deceitful possession of the object of my desire.

Many are the delicious things, Nathaniel, for which I have been consumed with love. Their splendour came from my ceaseless burning for them. I never wearied. All fervour consumed me with love – consumed me deliciously.

A heretic among heretics, I was constantly drawn to the most opposite opinions, the most devious thoughts, the extremest divergencies. Nothing interested me in a mind but what made it different from others. I went so far as to forbid myself sympathy, which seemed to me the mere recognition of a common emotion.

No, not sympathy, Nathaniel – love.

Act without *judging* whether the action is right or wrong.
Love without caring whether what you love is good or bad.
Nathaniel, I will teach you fervour.
A harrowing life, Nathaniel, rather than a quiet one. Let me

have no rest but the sleep of death. I am afraid that every desire, every energy I have not satisfied in life may survive to torment me. I hope that after I have expressed on this earth all that was in me waiting to be expressed – I *hope* that I may die satisfied and utterly *hopeless*.

No, not sympathy, Nathaniel, Love. Surely you understand they are not the same? It was the fear of wasting love that made me sometimes sympathize with sorrows, troubles, sufferings which else I could hardly have borne. Leave to each one the care of his own life.

(I cannot write today because a wheel is turning in the barn. Yesterday I saw it; it was thrashing colza.

The chaff blew away; the grain rolled on to the floor.

The dust was suffocating.

A woman was turning the mill-stone. Two handsome bare-footed boys were collecting the grain.

And here I am crying because I have nothing else to say.

I know one ought not to begin writing when one has nothing else than that to say. And yet I have written more – I shall write more again on the same subject.)

*   *

*

Nathaniel, I should like to bestow on you a joy no-one else has ever bestowed. I do not know how to bestow it and yet that joy is mine. I should like to speak to you more intimately than anyone has ever yet spoken to you. I should like to come to you at that hour of the night when you have opened, one after the other and then shut, a great many books – after looking in each one of them for something more than it has ever told you; when you are still expectant; when your fervour is about to turn into sadness for want of sustenance. I write only for you, and for you only in those hours. I should like to write a book from which every thought, every emotion of my own would seem to you absent, in which you would see nothing but the projection of your own fervour. I should like to draw near you and make you *love* me.

Melancholy is nothing but abated fervour.

Every creature is capable of nakedness and every emotion of plenitude.

My emotions flowered in me like a divine revelation. Can you understand this – that every emotion is *present* – infinitely?

Nathaniel, I will teach you fervour.

Our acts are attached to us as its glimmer is to phosphorus. They consume us, it is true, but they make our splendour.

And if our souls have been of any worth, it is because they have burnt more ardently than others.

Great fields, washed in the whiteness of dawn, I have seen you; blue lakes, I have bathed in your waters – and to every caress of the laughing breeze I have smiled back an answer – this is what I shall never tire of telling you, Nathaniel. I will teach you fervour.

If I had known more lovely things than these, it is of them that I should have told you – yes, yes, of them and not of any others.

You have not taught me wisdom, Menalcas.
'Not wisdom, but love.'

*   *
*

I felt for Menalcas more than friendship, Nathaniel, and hardly less than love. I loved him too as a brother.

Menalcas is dangerous; beware of him; wise men condemn him, but children are not afraid of him. He weans them from loving nothing but their own family, and teaches them to leave it slowly; he makes their hearts sick with longing for fruit that is wild and sour, with curiosity for strange loves. Ah, Menalcas! I would gladly have travelled with you along many another path. But you hated weakness, and your proud claim was to teach me to leave you.

There are strange possibilities in every man. The present would be pregnant with all futures, if it had not been already informed with its history by the past. But alas, a one and only past can offer us no more than a one and only future, which it casts before us like an infinite bridge over space.

We can only be sure of never doing what we are incapable of understanding. To understand is to feel capable of doing. ASSUME AS MUCH HUMANITY AS POSSIBLE —let this be your motto.

Manifold forms of life! One and all, how beautiful I thought you! (This that I am saying to you is what Menalcas said to me.)

Indeed I hope that I have known all passions and all vices; at any rate I have favoured them. I have been passionately drawn to all creeds; and on certain evenings I was mad enough almost to believe in my soul, I felt it so near escaping from my body. (Menalcas said this too.)

And our life will have been set before us like that glass of iced water, that moist glass which a sick man holds in his feverish hands, which he longs to drink, which he drinks at one draught, knowing that he ought to wait, but incapable of putting aside that delicious glass from his lips, so cool is the water, so hotly his fever pants for it.

II

Ah, how deeply I have inhaled the cold night air, ah, casements! And you, pale beams, streaming from the moon through the mists of night, so like water from a spring – one seemed to drink you!

Ah, casements! How often I have cooled my brow against your panes, and how often, when I sprang from the unbearable heat of my bed and ran to the balcony, my desires vanished like a wraith at sight of the vast and tranquil skies!

Fevers of bygone days, you consumed my flesh with a mortal consumption; but how great is the soul's exhaustion when nothing distracts it from God!

The fixity of my adoration was fearful. I was absorbed in it to self-extinction.

'You would search long,' said Menalcas, 'for the impossible happiness of the soul.'

After the first days of dubious ecstasy had gone by – but before I met Menalcas – I went through a period of anxiety, of suspense. It was like crossing a bog. I sank overwhelmed into heavy slumbers of which no amount of sleep sufficed to cure me. I lay down after my meals and slept. I woke up more tired than before, with a mind benumbed, as though in the first stages of a metamorphosis. Obscure operations of life; latent travail, unknown births awaiting their genesis, laborious deliveries; drowsiness, passivity; I slept like a chrysalis and a pupa; I let the new, already different creature I was going to be, form within me. All light reached me as though filtered through a depth upon depth of green waters, through leaves and branches. My perceptions were as confused and deadened as those of a stunned or drunken man. 'Ah!' I prayed, 'let the crisis come to a head now, at once, let the disease declare itself, the pain stab me!' And my brain felt like those stormy skies, charged with lowering clouds, on days when to breathe is almost impossible, and all nature longs for the flash of lightning which will rip open the murky, humour-laden bladders that blot out Heaven's azure.

How long, how long, O waiting, will you last? And once over, what will there be left to live for? 'Waiting! Longing! For what?' I cried. 'What can come that is not born of ourselves? And what can be born of us that we do not know already?'

Abel's birth, my betrothal, Eric's death – all this upheaval of my life, far from putting an end to my apathy, seemed to plunge me still deeper into it, so that my torpor seemed to come from the very complexity of my thought and indecision of my will. I should have liked to sleep to all eternity in the moisture of the earth, like a vegetable. Sometimes I said to myself that sensual pleasure would put an end to my trouble, and tried to liberate my mind by exhausting my flesh. Then I went to sleep again for hour after hour, like small children who feel drowsy with the heat and are put to bed at noon in the stir of a bustling household.

Then, called back from Heaven knows where, I woke up in

a sweat, with a beating heart and a numbed brain. The light that trickled in from below through the cracks of the closed shutters and cast green reflections of the lawn on to the white ceiling – that evening light was my one solace; it was soft and charming as the glimmer that filters through leaves and water and trembles on the threshold of dim grottoes, to eyes long accustomed to their glooms.

The household noises reached me vaguely. Slowly I came back to life. I washed in warm water and went languidly down to the plain, as far as the garden bench, where in utter idleness I waited for the evening to draw in. I was perpetually too tired to speak, to listen, to write. I read:

> '... He sees before him
> The deserted roads, the sea-gulls
> As they spread their wings and bathe ...
> It is here that I must live ...
> ... I am forced to dwell
> Under the leaves of the forest,
> Under the oak-trees
> In this underground cave.
> Cold is this earthy house;
> I am weary of it;
> Gloomy the valleys,
> High the hills.
> Sad dwelling, set round with branches,
> Roofed with brambles –
> Cheerless abode.'[1]

The feeling that a plenitude of life was possible, though not yet achieved, sometimes came in glimpses, then oftener, then more and more insistently, hauntingly. 'Ah!' I cried, 'let a breach be thrown open, let the daylight come flooding in, let it shine at last among these perpetual peevish glooms!'

My whole being felt, as it were, an immense need to refresh its vigour in a bath of newness. I awaited a second puberty. Ah! if only my eyes could see with new vision! If only I could cleanse them from the soil of books, make them more like the

1. *The Exile's Song.* Translated from the Anglo-Saxon by Taine and quoted in *Littérature Anglaise*, Vol. I, p. 30.

skies they look at – skies which today have been washed bright and clean by the recent rains. . . .

I fell ill; I travelled, I met Menalcas, and my marvellous convalescence was a palingenesis. I was born again with a new self, in a new country, and amongst things which were absolutely fresh.

III

Nathaniel, I will speak to you of waiting – expecting – longing. (If I had one word to express this threefold meaning I would use it.)

I have seen the plains in summer waiting – expecting – longing for a little rain. The dust on the roads had become so light that a breath raised it. It was not even longing – it was apprehension. The earth had cracked into great fissures from the drought, as though better to welcome the coming water. The scent of the wild moorland flowers was almost intolerable, and the world lay gasping in the heat of the sun. Every afternoon we went to rest below the terrace, where we were a little sheltered from the extreme fierceness of the light. It was that time of year when the cone-bearing trees are laden with pollen and gently wave their branches in order to scatter their fertilizing dust abroad. Storm clouds had piled themselves in the lowering sky and all nature was expectant. The moment was oppressively solemn, for the birds had fallen silent. So hot a breath rose from the earth that all life seemed to be swooning, and the pollen from the trees floated from the branches like a golden smoke. Then it rained.

I have seen the sky shiver as it waited for dawn. One by one the stars faded. The meadows were flooded with dew; no caress of the air's but was icy. It seemed to me that the indistinguishable throb of life all around me was lingering, reluctant to awake, and my head too was heavy with torpor. I climbed to the outskirts of the wood; I sat down; the creatures, confident in the return of day, resumed their labours and their joys, and the mystery of life began once more to rustle in the fretwork of the leaves – then the day dawned.

I have seen still other dawns. I have seen the night too, awaited, longed for.

But, Nathaniel, let your waiting be not even a longing, but simply a welcoming. Welcome everything that comes to you, but do not long for anything else. Long only for what you have. Understand that at every moment of the day God in His entirety may be yours. Let your longing be love and your possession a lover's. For what is a longing that is not effectual?

What, Nathaniel, you possess God, without being aware of it! To possess God is to see Him, but you do not look. Balaam, did you not see God who stood in your way and from whom your ass turned aside? Because *you* had imagined Him otherwise.

Nathaniel, God only must not be awaited. Who awaits God, Nathaniel, fails to understand he possesses Him. Believe that God and happiness are one, and put all your happiness in the present moment.

As women in the pale East wear their entire fortune on their persons, so I have always carried with me all my possessions. At every smallest moment of my life, I have felt within me the whole of my wealth. It consisted, not of the addition of a great many particular items, but of my single adoration of them. I have constantly carried my whole wealth in my whole power.

Look upon the evening as the death of the day; and upon the morning as the birth of all things.

Let every moment renew your vision.

The wise man is he who constantly wonders afresh.

All the weariness of your mind, O Nathaniel, comes from the diversity of your possessions. You do not even know which of them all you prefer and you cannot understand that the only possession of any value is life. The smallest moment of life is stronger than death and cancels it. Death is no more than permission granted to other modes of life to exist – so that everything may be ceaselessly renewed – so that no mode of life may last longer than the time needed for it to express itself. Happy the moment in which your words resound. In other moments, listen; but when you speak, listen no longer.

You must make a bonfire in your heart, Nathaniel, of all your books.

A LAY

WORSHIPPING WHAT I HAVE BURNT

Some books one reads sitting on a narrow bench
In front of a school desk.

Some books one reads out walking
(A little too because of their size);
Some are for the woods,
Some for other country places –
Nobiscum rusticantur, *says Cicero.*

There are some I have read in diligences;
Some others lying in a hay-loft.
There are some that make us believe in the existence of the
                    soul;
Others that make us despair of it.
Some that prove there is a God;
Others that fail to.

Some that can only be admitted into private libraries;
Some that have been praised by many eminent critics.

There are some that treat of nothing but apiculture
And might be thought a little technical;
Others in which there is so much talk of nature,
That after reading them there is no need to go out for a walk.

There are some that are despised by wise men
But that thrill little children.

26

Some are called anthologies
And contain all the best sayings
On everything under the sun.
There are some that try to make one love life;
Others, after writing which
The author has committed suicide.
There are some that sow hatred
And reap what they have sown.
Some, as one reads them, seem to shine,
Charged with ecstasy, delicious with humility.
There are some one loves like brothers
Who have lived more purely and better than we.
There are some written in such strange languages
That even after a deep study of them,
They are impossible to understand.

Nathaniel, when shall we make a bonfire of all our books?

Some there are not worth a penny-piece;
Others extremely valuable.
Some speak of kings and queens,
And others of the very poor.

There are some whose words are sweeter
Than the rustle of leaves at noon.
It was a book that John ate on Patmos,
Like a rat, (as for me, I prefer raspberries);
It made his belly bitter
And afterwards he had visions.

A bonfire, Nathaniel, of all our books ! ! !

It is not enough for me to *read* that the sand on the seashore is soft. My bare feet must feel it. I have no use for knowledge that has not been preceded by a sensation.

I have never seen anything sweetly beautiful in this world without desiring to touch it with all my fondness. O lovely surface of the earth, how marvellous is your flowering! Scenes into whose heart my desire plunges, lands lying open before me which my longing explores! Papyrus alley, growing over water, reeds bending down to the river, glades opening out in the forest, visions of the plain through an embrasure of branches, visions of unbounded promise! I have walked in narrow passages through rocks or plants. I have seen springs unfold — FLUIDITY OF PHENOMENA.

From that day onward every moment brought me its freshness as an ineffable gift, so that I lived in an almost perpetual state of passionate wonder. I became intoxicated with extreme rapidity and went about in a sort of daze.

Yes, I have always desired to kiss the laughter I have seen on happy lips, to drink the blood of blushing cheeks, the tears of filling eyes; to put my teeth into the flesh of every fruit from the branches that dangled above me. At every inn a hunger greeted me; at every spring a thirst awaited me — a different thirst at every spring; and I wanted other words to express my other desires

of walking where a path lay open;
of resting where the shade invited;
of swimming where the waters were deep;
of loving or sleeping in every bed that offered.

I have boldly laid my hands where I wished, and believed I had a right to every object of my desires. (And besides, what we want, Nathaniel, is not so much possession as love.) Ah! wherever I go, may all things be irradiated with brightness! May all beauty be clothed and coloured with my love!

BOOK II

FOOD!
  I demand you, food!
  My hunger will stay at no half-way house;
  Nothing but satisfaction will silence it;
  No moralities can put an end to it,
  And I have never fed anything but my soul on privations.

  Satisfactions! I seek you.
  You are beautiful as summer dawns.

  Springs, so sweet in the evening, more delicious still at
noon; icy waters of early morning; breezes blowing from
the sea; bays crowded with shipping; warm, wave-lapped
shores . . .
  Oh! if there still are roads that lead towards the plains, let
them bring me to hot gusts of noon and country drinks and at
night the hollowed haystack;
  if any roads lead Eastwards – the wake of ships through beloved seas, gardens at Mossul, dances at Touggourt and songs
of shepherd lads in Helvetia;
  if any roads lead Northwards – fairs at Nijni, snow-
spattering sledges and frozen lakes. No fear, Nathaniel, that
our desires will grow stale.
  Here are boats come to our harbours, bringing ripe fruit
from unknown lands!
  Quick! Quick! Unload them of their freight, so that at last
we may taste it.

  Food!
  I demand you, food!
  Satisfactions, I seek you;
  You are beautiful as summer's laughter.
  I know that not one of my desires
  But has its own answer ready.

Its reward awaits each one of my hungers.
Food!
I demand you, food!
Throughout all space, I seek you,
Satisfactions of all my desires!

*   *
*

The most beautiful thing I have known on earth,
Ah! Nathaniel, is my hunger.
It has always been faithful
To all that has always awaited it.
Is it on wine that the nightingale gets drunk?
Or the eagle on milk? And the thrush, is it not on juniper
berries?
The eagle is drunk with its flight. The nightingale with
summer nights. The plains tremble with their heat. Nathaniel,
let every one of your emotions be an intoxication to you. If
what you eat fails to make you drunk, it can only be that you
were not hungry enough.

Every perfect action is accompanied by pleasure. That is
how you can tell that it was right for you to do it. I don't like
people who pride themselves on working painfully. If their
work was painful, they had better have done something else.
The delight one takes in one's work is the sign of its fitting-
ness, and the sincerity of my pleasure, Nathaniel, is my chief
guide.

I know the daily capacity of my body for pleasure and how
much of it my mind can bear. And then sleep will begin.
Heaven and earth are of no further use to me.

There are extravagant illnesses
Which consist in wanting what one hasn't got.

'We too,' they said, 'we too have known that lamentable
sickness of the soul!' In the cave of Adullam, David, you

sighed for other waters. 'Oh, who will bring me,' you sighed, 'the cool water that gushes from the foot of the walls of Bethlehem? As a child, I quenched my thirst at it; but now it runs captive – that water my fever pants for.'

Never long, Nathaniel, to taste the waters of the past.

Never seek, Nathaniel, to find again the past in the future. Seize from every moment its unique novelty and never prepare your joys – or else believe that in its proper place *another* joy will be there to surprise you.

Oh, why have you not understood that all happiness is a chance encounter and at every moment stands beside you like a beggar by the roadside. Woe betide you if you say your happiness is dead because you had not imagined it in that form – and because you will only accept a happiness in conformity with your principles and wishes.

Your dream of tomorrow is a delight – but tomorrow will have another delight of its own, and nothing fortunately is like the dream we have dreamt of it, for each thing has a *special and different value*.

I don't like you to say, 'Come, I have prepared such or such a joy for you.' I only care now for the joys that meet me by the roadside and for those that spring at my bidding from the rocks; for thus they flow for us fresh and strong, as new wine when it gushes from the press.

I don't want my joy to be dressed up for me, nor the Shulamite to come to me through palace halls; I kissed her without wiping the stains of grape-juice from my lips; after my kisses, I drank sweet wine without rinsing my mouth, and I ate honey with its comb.

Nathaniel, never prepare your joys.

* *
*

When you cannot say, 'Very good!' say, 'Never mind!' That way lies the promise of much happiness.

Some people think their moments of happiness are given them by God – and others that they are given by – Whom?

33

Nathaniel, do not distinguish between your happiness and God.

I can no more be grateful to 'God' for having created me than I could be resentful towards Him for not existing – if I did not exist.

Nathaniel, you should only speak of God naturally.

I agree that if once the fact of existence is granted, the existence of the earth and mankind and myself may seem natural. But what confounds and amazes my intelligence is that I should be aware of it.

No doubt I too have sung hymns, and once I wrote a

LAY

ON THE FINEST PROOFS OF THE EXISTENCE OF GOD

You must know, Nathaniel, that the finest poetical flights are those that treat of the thousand and one proofs of the existence of God. Of course you understand that I have no intention of repeating them here, and still less of simply repeating them – and then some of them only prove His existence, and what we want is also the proof of its permanence.

Oh yes, I know, there is St Anselm's argument,
And the apologue of the Fortunate Isles.
But alas, alas, Nathaniel, everyone can't live in them.

I know there is the opinion of the many.
But you believe in the fitness of the few.

There is, of course, the proof by two and two make four. –
But, Nathaniel, we aren't all good at arithmetic.

There is the proof of the First Cause. –
But there is always another that came before it.
It's a pity, Nathaniel, we weren't there at the beginning.
We should have seen the creation of the first man and the first woman,
And their astonishment at not having been born infants;

34

And the cedars of Elbrouz, already weary by having been born hundreds of years old
And on mountains already furrowed by the rain.
Oh, Nathaniel! To have been there for the first dawn! —
How did we come to be such sluggards? Weren't you longing to be alive? Ah! I am sure I was . . . But the spirit of God was barely waking then, after having brooded on the waters in timeless abysses. If I had been there, Nathaniel, I should have asked him to make everything a little bigger; and don't you say that then it wouldn't have been noticeable.[1]

There is the proof by final causes.
But not everyone thinks that the end justifies the means.

Some people prove God by the love they feel for Him. That is why, Nathaniel, I have called everything I have loved God, and why I have determined to love everything. Don't be alarmed; I am not going to make a list, and in any case, I shouldn't begin with you; I have preferred many things to men, and they are by no means what I have most loved on earth. For make no mistake, Nathaniel, my heart is certainly not the strongest part of me, nor even, I think, the best; and it is not their heart that I esteem most in men. Nathaniel, put your God before them. I too have praised God; I have sung hymns to Him — and I even think I have sometimes slightly overdone it.

'Do you find it so very amusing,' he said, 'to construct all these systems?'

'I find nothing,' I answered, 'more amusing than a system of ethics, nor more satisfying to my mind. I want every single joy I taste to be attached to one.'

'Does that increase it?'

'No,' I said, 'but it allows me to think it legitimate.'

True, I have often been glad to justify my acts to myself by a doctrine, and even by a complete system of ordered thought;

---

1. 'I can perfectly imagine another world,' said Alcides, 'in which two and two wouldn't make four.'
'The deuce you can!' said Menalcas.

but at other times, I could not help suspecting that I was merely providing a shelter for my sensuality.

*　　*
*

Everything comes at its own hour, Nathaniel; everything is born of its need and is merely, so to speak, the outward expression of a need.

'I needed lungs,' said the tree, 'and my sap turned to leaves so that I might breathe. Then when I had breathed, my leaves fell and I did not die. My fruit contains all my thoughts on life.'

Don't be afraid, Nathaniel, that I shall overdo this form of apologue, for I don't much approve of it. The only wisdom I want to teach you is life. For thinking is a heavy burden. I exhausted myself when I was young by following the results of actions as far as I could into the future, and I was never sure of not sinning save by not acting.

Then I wrote: 'I owed the health of my body only to the irremediable poisoning of my soul.' Then I ceased to understand what I had meant by this.

Nathaniel, I no longer believe in sin.

But you must understand that it takes a great deal of joy to purchase a little right to think. He who counts himself happy and who yet thinks, he shall be called the true worthy.

Nathaniel, our misfortune is that it is always we who look and that we subordinate what we see to ourselves. It is not for us but for itself that each thing is important. Let your eye be the thing it looks at.

Nathaniel, I cannot write a single line now, without your delicious name beginning it.

Nathaniel, I want to bring you to life.

Nathaniel, do you really feel the poignancy of my words? I want to get nearer to you still.

And as Elisha stretched himself upon the Shulamite's son to recall him to life – 'his mouth upon his mouth, and his eyes

36

upon his eyes, and his hands upon his hands,' so will I, shedding all the light of my radiant heart upon your still unilluminated soul, stretch myself upon you, my mouth upon your mouth, my forehead upon your forehead, your cold hands in my burning hands, and my beating heart ... ('And,' it is written, 'the flesh of the child waxed warm' ...) so that you may awake in delight – *and then leave me* – for a thrilling and lawless life.

Nathaniel, here is all the warmth of my soul – take it.

Nathaniel, I would teach you fervour.

Nathaniel, never stay with what is like you. Never *stay* anywhere. When your surroundings have taken on your likeness, or you yourself have grown like your surroundings, they have ceased to profit you. You must leave them. There is no greater danger for you than your own family, your own room, your own past. Take from each thing nothing but what it teaches you; and let the pleasure that streams from it drain it dry.

Nathaniel, I must speak to you of *moments*. Do you realize the power of their *presence*? A not sufficiently constant thought of death has given an insufficient value to the tiniest moment of your life. Don't you understand that the moment would not take on such incomparable vividness, if it were not thrown up, so to speak, on the dark background of death?

I should make no further attempt to do anything at all, if I were told, if it were proved to me that I had unlimited time to do it in. I should begin by resting from the effort of making up my mind to do something, if I had time enough to do everything else *as well*. I should always do no matter what, if I did not know there was an end to this form of life – and that when I have lived it out, I shall rest in a sleep a little deeper, a litttle more forgetful than the one I look forward to every night ...

*   *

*

In this way, I fell into the habit of *separating* each moment of my life in order to fill it wholly with a complete and isolated joy; in order suddenly to concentrate in it a special particularity of happiness; so that I could hardly recognize myself from one minute to the next.

*　　*
*

There is great pleasure, Nathaniel, in just simply making a plain statement – as for instance:

The fruit of the palm-tree is called *date*, and it makes a delicious food.

The wine of the palm-tree is called *lagmy*; it is made with the tree's fermented sap; the Arabs get drunk on it, and personally, I don't much care for it. It was a bowl of lagmy that the Kabyle shepherd offered me in the gardens of Ouardi.

*　　*
*

This morning, as I was walking in the grounds of Les Sources, I found an extraordinary mushroom.

It was like an orange-red magnolia fruit, sheathed in white and with regular markings on it, obviously made by a sporaginous powder coming from its inside. I opened it; it was full of a stuff like mud which towards the centre formed a transparent jelly; it gave out a sickly smell.

Near it were other mushrooms, which were wider opened and merely looked like those flattened fungoid growths one sees on the trunks of old trees.

(I wrote this before starting for Tunis; and I copy it out here to show you the importance every single thing took on for me as soon as I looked at it.)

*　　*
*

(*Honfleur in the street*).

And sometimes I felt as if other people round about me were moving and gesticulating merely in order to give me an increased sense of my own life.

Yesterday I was here; today I am there;
Oh dear! what do I care
For those who say, and say, and say,
Yesterday I was here, today I am there . . .

There were days when simply repeating to myself that two and two still made four was enough to fill me with positive beatitude – and the mere sight of my fist on the table . . . and other days when it was completely indifferent to me.

BOOK III

Villa Borghese.

IN this stone basin ... (dusk of shadowed light) ... every drop, every ray, every creature, passed away to death in voluptuous pleasure.

Pleasure! I should like to repeat that word incessantly; I should like it to be synonymous with well-being, and even that the simple word *being* should imply it.

Ah! that God should not have created the world with this sole purpose in view is impossible to understand, except by saying ... etc.

This place is exquisitely cool, and the charm of sleep here is so great that one seems never to have known it before.

Here too there was delicious food awaiting us, when we should be hungry for it.

The Adriatic (3 a.m.).

The song of the sailors in the rigging is exasperating.

O earth! so excessively old and so young, if you knew, if you only knew the bitter-sweet taste, the delicious taste of man's brief life!

If you only knew, eternal Idea of Phenomena, the value bestowed upon each moment by the near expectation of death!

O spring! the plants that live for only a single year hasten the flowering of their fragile blooms. Man has only a single spring in his life, and the memory of a past joy is not the herald of coming happiness.

Fiesole.

Beautiful Florence! City of learning, luxury and flowers; serious above all things; seed of myrtle and crown of 'slender laurel.[1]'

1. Goethe, *Tasso*, Act I, Sc. 1:
    'Du hast ...
    Den zarten, schlanken Lorbeer dir gewählt.'
    (Translator's note.)

Vincigliata. It was there I first saw clouds dissolving in the blue sky; it astonished me greatly, for I had no idea they could melt into the azure in this way, and had always thought they went on getting heavier and heavier, until they turned into rain. But no; I watched them disappearing, cloudlet after cloudlet, until nothing was left but the azure. It was a marvellous death – a vanishing in the midst of Heaven.

Rome, Monte Pincio.

The essence of my joy that day was something like love – but it was not love – or at any rate not the love men seek and speak of. It was not the sense of beauty either. It was not a woman who gave it me, nor yet my thoughts. Shall I venture to write, will you understand me if I say that it was nothing but glorified LIGHT?

I was sitting in this garden; I did not see the sun, but the air was shining with such an effusion of light that it seemed as if the blueness of the sky had turned liquid and was raining. Yes, really, there were ripples and eddies of light; on the moss there were sparkles like drops; yes, really, it seemed as though a river of light were flowing down the broad pathway, and golden spray had been left on the tips of the branches by this rushing stream of sunshine.

*

Naples; the barber's little shop, facing the sea and the sun. Sweltering quays; you lift the blind and step in. You let yourself go. How long will it last? Quietness. Drops of sweat on your temples. Tickling of lather on your cheeks. And the barber refines upon his shaving, when he has finished – goes on shaving with an ever skilfuller blade, and now, with the help of a little sponge soaked in warm water, he relaxes the skin and lifts the upper lip. Then he washes the smart with a gently perfumed lotion, and after that, soothes it again with an emollient cream. And in order to put off stirring for just a little longer, I tell him to cut my hair.

One waits at night – for what?

What love? Who knows?

A little room over the sea. I was woken up by the extreme brightness of the moon – the moon over the sea.

When I went to the window, I thought it was the dawn and that I was going to see the sunrise. . . . But no . . . (already full and perfectly accomplished) – it was the Moon – soft, soft, soft, as for the welcoming of Helen in the Second Faust. A deserted sea. A dead village. A dog howling in the night. . . . Rags hanging from some of the windows.

What place is there for man? How can any of all this ever wake up again? Utter desolation of the dog. There will never be another day. Impossible to sleep. What shall I do now – this or that?

> go out into the deserted garden?
> go down to the beach and bathe?
> go and pick those oranges that look grey in the moon-light?
> go and comfort the howling dog?

(I have so often felt that nature required some act of me, without my being able to guess which one I ought to give her.)

Shall I wait for sleep that will not come? . . .

A small boy followed me into the walled garden, helping himself down by clinging to the branches that brushed the steps. The steps led to terraces and ran alongside the garden which looked as if it would be impossible to get into.

O little face I caressed in the shadow of the leaves! No shade could have dimmed your brightness – and dark and darker still was the shadow of the curls on your brow.

I will go down into the garden, clinging as I go to the creepers and branches, and there sob out my heart in those bird-haunted groves, fuller of song than any aviary – until evening draws in, until night comes to gild and then to darken and deepen the mysterious water of the fountains.

Soft bodies close-wedded under the branches.
Soft touch of my fingers on his pearly skin.
Soft feet I watched treading silently on the sand.

Syracuse.

A flat-bottomed boat; a low sky, dropping on us at times in warm rain; the muddy smell of water-plants, the rustle of their stalks.

The water is so deep that the welling of its blue spring is imperceptible. No noise; in this solitary place, in this natural hollow of its basin, the water seems to be blossoming among the papyrus.

Tunis.

Amidst all this blue, there is only just enough white for a sail, only just enough green for its shadow in the water.

Night. Rings glitter in the dark.

One wanders in the moonlight. One's thoughts are different from daytime thoughts.

Sinister light of the moon in the desert. Demons prowl in the cemeteries. Bare feet on blue tiles.

Malta.

Strange intoxication of summer twilights in the open places of the town, when it is still very light and yet there are no shadows. A very special kind of excitement.

Nathaniel, I will tell you about the most beautiful gardens I have ever seen.

In Florence, roses were being sold in the streets; there were days when the whole town was perfumed with them. Every evening I walked in the Cascine and on Sundays in the Boboli gardens where there were no flowers.

In Seville, near the Giralda, there is an old courtyard in a mosque; orange-trees grow in part of it, symmetrically planted; the rest of the court is paved; on very sunny days, there is only a tiny streak of shade to be found in it; it is a square court, surrounded with walls and extremely beautiful; I can't explain why.

Outside the town, in a vast garden enclosed by iron railings, there are a great many tropical trees growing. I didn't go into it, but looked through the railings; I saw a number of guinea-fowls running about inside, and supposed it must be full of tame animals.

What of the Alcazar? Marvellous as a Persian garden! Now I come to speak of it, I believe I prefer it to all the others. When I read Hafiz, I think of it.

> *'Bring me wine*
> *So that I may stain my dress,*
> *For I reel with love*
> *And men call me wise.'*

Jets of water play beside the paths; the paths are paved with marble and bordered with myrtle and cypress. On each side are marble pools where the king's concubines bathed. The only flowers are roses, narcissus and oleander. At the end of the garden is a gigantic tree. One imagines a bulbul stuck in it. Near the place there are other pools in very bad taste which remind one of those in the courtyards of the Munich Residency, where there are statues entirely made of shells.

It was in the Royal gardens of Munich that one spring I tasted Maitrink ices, while an obstinate military band was playing near by. The public was dowdy but musical. The pathos of the nightingales gave enchantment to the evening. Their song lulled me into languor like German poetry. There is a certain intensity of delight which can hardly be surpassed by man – or not without tears. The very delights of those gardens made me think almost painfully that I might just as well have been somewhere else. It was during that summer that I learnt to appreciate more especially the pleasures of *temperature*. One's eyelids are admirably adapted to this purpose. I remember a night in a train which I spent beside an open window, solely taken up with the enjoyment of feeling the fresh air. I shut my eyes – not to sleep, but just for this *feeling*. The heat had been stifling all day, and that evening the air, though still warm, poured like a cool liquid on my inflamed eyelids.

At Granada, the terraces of the Generaliffe, which are planted with oleanders, were not in flower when I saw them; nor was the Campo Santo of Pisa, nor the little cloisters of San Marco, which I should have liked to see full of roses. But at Rome, I saw the Pincio at the best time of year. In the sultry afternoons people used to go there in search of coolness, and as I lived near by, I went to walk in the gardens every day. I was ill and incapable of thinking; nature just sank into me; thanks to some nervous disorder, my body seemed at times to have no limits; it was prolonged outside myself – or sometimes became porous; I felt myself deliciously melting away, like sugar. Rome, the sight of which fatigued me intolerably, was not visible from where I used to sit, on a stone bench overlooking the Borghese gardens. The slope of the ground put the distant tops of their tallest pine-trees on a level with my feet. O terraces! Terraces, whence space itself is launched. O aerial navigation! . . .

I should have liked to roam about in the Farnese gardens at night; but one isn't allowed in. The vegetation with which the ruins are overgrown and concealed is wonderful.

At Naples, there are low-lying gardens along the seashore, like quays; the sunshine floods them:

at Nîmes, the Fountain, fed by channels of clear water;

at Montpellier, the Botanical gardens. I remember one evening sitting there with Ambrose (as it might have been in the gardens of Academia) on an ancient tomb, planted round with cypress; we munched rose-petals as we conversed slowly.

One night, at Le Peyrou, we saw the moon-silvered sea in the distance; the noise of rushing water from the town's water-tower sounded in our ears close by; there were black swans fringed with white, swimming in the still garden pool.

At Malta, I used to read in the Residency gardens; there was a tiny little wood of lemon-trees at Cita Vecchia; it was called 'il Boschetto'; we liked going there; we used to pick the ripe lemons and bite them; their juice at first is intolerably sour, but afterwards it leaves a refreshing perfume in the mouth. We tasted some at Syracuse too, in the cruel Latomie.

At the Hague, there are deer running wild in the park – not very wild.

From the gardens of Avranche one can see St Michael's Mount; in the evening the distant sands look incandescent.

Some very small towns have charming gardens; one forgets the town; one forgets its name; one would like to revisit the garden but it is impossible to find it.

I dream of the gardens of Mossul; I am told they are full of roses. The gardens of Najpur have been sung by Omar, and those of Shiraz by Hafiz; we shall never see the gardens of Najpur.

But at Biskra, I know the gardens of Ouardi with their boy goatherds.

At Tunis, the only garden is the cemetery. At Algiers, in the Botanical gardens (palm-trees of every species), I ate fruits I had never seen before. And Blidah! O Nathaniel, what shall I say of Blidah?

Ah! tender the grass of the Sahel! And your orange-blossom! and your shade! And sweet the scent of your gardens! Blidah! Blidah! Little rose! At the beginning of winter I misjudged you. The only leaves in your sacred grove were those that no spring renews; your creepers, your wistaria, looked like dry sticks for burning. The mountain snow had drifted near you; I couldn't keep warm in my room, and still less in your rainy gardens. I spent the time reading Fichte's *Doctrine of Science*, and felt myself becoming religious again. I was all meekness; one must resign oneself, I said, to one's sadness, and I tried to make a virtue out of this state. Now I have shaken the dust of my sandals upon it. Who knows whither the wind has blown it? Dust of the desert, where I wandered like a prophet; parched and powdered stone, how burning I felt it to my feet (for the sun had baked it). Now let my feet rest in the grass of the Sahel! Let all our words be of love!

Blidah! Blidah! Flower of the Sahel! Little rose! I saw you once again in your warmth and fragrance, full of leaves and flowers. Winter's snows had fled. In the sacred grove your white mosque glimmered mystically and the creepers were bowed down with flowers. An olive-tree was half hidden under the garlands a wistaria had made for it. A gentle breeze wafted me the perfume of the orange blossoms and even the tangerines smelt deliciously. From the tallest of their topmost branches the eucalyptus trees, free once more, shed their last year's bark; it hung in tatters, a worn-out covering, like a garment made useless by the sun, like my old morals, which were only serviceable in winter.

Blidah.

The huge stalks of fennel (a blaze of green and gold in the golden sunlight or under the azure-tinted leaves of the motionless eucalyptus) shone with incomparable splendour that morning of early summer on our road through the Sahel.
Were the eucalyptus-trees astounded or placid?

There is nothing that does not participate in nature. Impossibility of escape. All-embracing laws of nature. The carriage that speeds through the night, in the morning is wet with dew.

On board.

How many nights, round window-pane of my cabin, O closed port-hole! how many nights, lying in my berth, have I looked towards you and thought: Ah! when that eye begins to whiten, it will be dawn; then I shall get up and shake off my sickness; and dawn will wash the sea, and we shall land on the Terra Incognita. – But dawn came without calming the sea; the land was still distant and on the moving face of the waters my mind still swayed.

Heaving of the waves, felt unforgettably throughout one's flesh! Can I fasten a thought to that vacillating main-top? thought I. Waves, am I to see nothing but spin-drift blown in the evening wind? I cast my love upon the waters – my thoughts on the barren plain of the sea. My love dives into the waves of the sea – waves for ever passing, for ever the same. They pass on and the eye knows them no more. Formless, ever restless sea! Far from man, your waves are silent; nothing opposes their fluidity; but no-one can hear their silence; even the frailest skiff shatters them, and their noise makes us think the tempest noisy. The great waves pass on and succeed each other noiselessly. They follow each other and each in turn lifts the same drop of water and barely moves it from its place. Their form alone moves on; the water is lent them for a moment, then leaves them, accompanies them never. Form never dwells in the same being for more than a moment; it passes on through each being and then leaves it. Let there be no thought, my soul, to which you cling. Cast each one of your thoughts to the sea-winds and let them bear it from you. Your own efforts will never carry it up to Heaven.

Fluctuating waters! It was you who made my thoughts unsteady. Nothing can be built up on a wave; it gives beneath the slightest weight.

Will the quiet haven come at last, after all this wearisome drifting, these tossings to and fro? Will my soul rest at last on some solid pier, beside a flashing lighthouse, and from there look at the sea?

*

BOOK IV

*A garden on a Florentine
hill (facing Fiesole) – our
meeting place that evening.*

'But you do not, cannot know, Angaire, Ydier, Tityrus,' said
Menalcas (and I repeat you his words now, Nathaniel, in my
own name), 'the passion that devoured my youth. The flight
of time maddened me. The necessity of choice was always intolerable; choosing seemed to me not so much selecting as
rejecting what I didn't select. I realized with horror how res-
tricted were the passing hours and that time has only one
dimension – a line, I thought – whereas I wanted it deep and
wide; as my desires hurried impatiently along it, they inevitably impinged on each other. I never did anything but this *or*
that. If I did *this*, I immediately regretted *that*, and I often
remained motionless, not daring to do anything, but my arms
wide open in distraction, fearing to close them, lest it should
be to clasp only *one* thing. The mistake of my life in those days
was to be incapable of pursuing any study for long because I
could not make up my mind to give up a host of others. Anything was too dear at such a price, and no reasoning could re-
lieve my distress. To enter a market of delights with too small
a sum (thanks to Whom?) at my disposal. To spend it, to
choose, was to give up for ever any chance of the remainder,
and the innumerable quantity of that remainder always seemed
preferable to any single item whatever.

'This was the cause of some of the aversion I feel for any
possession on earth – the fear of immediately possessing nothing
but that.

'Merchandise! Stores of wealth! Heaps of treasure-trove!
Why can you not be given us unsparingly? I know, indeed,
that the produce of the earth is not inexhaustible (though inex-
haustibly renewable) and that the cup I have emptied remains

empty for you, my brother (though its source springs near at hand). But you, immaterial ideas! unappropriated forms of life! sciences of Nature and knowledge of God! cups of truth! cups that can never run dry! why do you grudge us your abundance, when all our thirst could never drain you, and you would overflow eternally with fresh water for the outstretched lips of every fresh comer? I have learnt now that all the drops of that divine fountain-head are equivalent; that the smallest suffices to transport us and reveals the plenitude and totality of God. But at that time, what did I not desire in my madness? I envied every form of life; everything I saw another do, I wanted to do myself — not to have done it, mind you, but to do it — for I had very little fear of fatigue or suffering, and believed them to be pregnant with instruction. I was jealous of Parmenides for three weeks on end because he was learning Turkish; two months later of Theodosius who had discovered astronomy. So that the figure I drew of myself was the vaguest and most uncertain, because I could not consent to limit it.'

'Tell us the story of your life, Menalcas,' said Alcides. And Menalcas went on:

'At eighteen years of age, when I had finished my first schooling, with a mind weary of work, an unoccupied heart sick of its own emptiness, and a body exasperated by constraint, I took to the road, with no end in view but simply to cool my vagabond fever. I experienced all the things you know so well — the springtime, the smell of the earth, the flowering of the fields, the mists of morning on the rivers, the haze of evening on the meadows. I passed through towns, but stopped nowhere. Happy, thought I, the man who is attached to nothing on earth and who carries his fervour unremittingly with him through all the ceaseless mobility of life. I hated homes and families and all the places where a man thinks to find rest; and lasting affections, and the fidelities of love, and attachment to ideas — all that endangers justice; I held that every new thing should always find the whole of us wholly available.

'Books had taught me that every liberty is provisional and never anything but the power to choose one's slavery, or at any rate one's devotion — as the thistle seed flies hither and thither, seeking a fertile soil in which to fix its roots – and can only flower when motionless. But as I had learnt at school that men are not guided by reasoning and that every argument may be opposed by a contrary one which needs only to be found, I set about looking for it, sometimes even in the course of my long journeyings.

'I lived in the perpetual, delicious expectation of the future – no matter what it might be. I taught myself that, like expectant questions in face of their answers, the thirst that arises in face of every pleasure must be swift to precede its enjoyment. My happiness came from this – that a thirst was revealed me by every spring and that in the waterless desert where thirst cannot be quenched, I preferred to it the fierceness of my fever, and the excitement of the sun. In the evenings, I came upon wonderful oases, all the cooler for having been so longed for during the day. On the sandy plain that lay stretched in the sun, as though struck down by a vast and overpowering sleep, I have still felt, so great was the heat and even in the very vibration of the air – I have still felt a pulsing life that could not sleep – I have felt it tremble and faint in the curve of the horizon, and at my feet grow big with love.

'Every day, and from hour to hour, I wanted nothing but to be more and more simply absorbed into nature. I possessed the precious gift of not being too greatly encumbered by myself. Remembrance of the past had only just enough power over me to give the necessary unity to my life – like the mysterious thread that bound Theseus to his past love but did not prevent him from pushing on to newer and still newer prospects. And even so, that thread too had to be broken. . . . Ah, wonderful palingenesis! Often in my early morning rambles, I have had the delicious sensation of having a new self, a fresh delicacy of perception. "The poet's gift," I cried, "is the gift of perpetual discovery," and I welcomed whatever came. My soul was the inn standing open at the cross-roads; entered whatever would. I made myself ductile, conciliatory; I was at the disposal of each one of my senses, attentive, a listener without a single thought of himself, a captor of every passing emotion, and so little capable of reaction that, rather than protest against anything, I preferred to think ill of nothing.

Indeed, I soon noticed how little my love of beauty was based upon hatred of ugliness.

'It was lassitude I hated, for I knew it was made of tedium, and I held that one should confidently reckon on the world's inexhaustible diversity. I took my rest no matter where. I have slept in the fields; I have slept in the woods. I have seen the dawn quivering between tall corn-sheaves, and the rooks awaking above beech groves. There were mornings when I washed in the grass and the rising sun dried my damp clothes. Was the country ever more beautiful than on the day I saw a rich harvest carried home to the sound of singing, and oxen drawing the big lumbering wagons?

'There came a time when my joy was so great that I longed to communicate it and teach someone else how I kept it so perennially alive.

'Sometimes in little obscure villages, I used to watch the homes that had been dispersed during the day coming together again in the evening; the father returning tired out from his work, the children from their school. For a moment the house-door would open on a glimpse of welcoming light and warmth and laughter, and then shut again for the night. No vagabond thing could enter now, no blast of the shivering wind outside. – Families, I hate you! closed circles round the hearth; fast shut doors; jealous possession of happiness. – Sometimes, invisible in the night, I stood leaning at the window-pane for a long space, watching the habits of a household. The father was there near the lamp; the mother sat sewing; the grandfather's chair stood empty; a boy was doing his lessons beside his father – and my heart swelled with the desire to take him away with me to live a wandering life on the roads.

'The next day I saw him coming out of school; the day after, I spoke to him; four days later, he left everything to follow me. I opened his eyes to the glory of the plains; he understood that it was for him their glory lay open. And so I taught his soul to become more vagabond – to become joyful – to free itself at last even from me – to grow acquainted with its solitude.

'Alone, I enjoyed the violent pleasure of pride. I liked to

rise before dawn; I called up the sun to shine on the stubble fields; the lark sang my fancies; the dew was my morning lotion. I took pleasure in excessive frugality and ate so little that my head grew light and the slightest sensation procured me a kind of drunkenness. I have drunk many wines since then, but I have known none of them give that intoxication that comes from fasting – that swimming of the plains in the early morning when, once the sun had risen, I fell asleep in the hollow of a haystack.

'I sometimes kept the bread I had taken with me till I was half fainting; then nature seemed to me less alien, more intimately penetrating – an influx from without, a presence welcomed by all my eager senses, a feast to which all within me was invited.

'My soul was in a state of lyrical ecstasy which my solitude enhanced and which grew fatiguing towards evening. I was kept up by pride, but at such times I regretted Hilary who the year before had shared and moderated the over-wildness of my moods.

'Towards evening I used to talk to him; he was a poet himself; he had an ear for harmonies. In every natural effect we could read its cause as in an open book; we learnt to recognize the insect by its flight, the bird by its song, and the beauty of women by their footprints in the sand. He too was devoured by a thirst for adventure; his strength had made him bold. Ah! no later glory will ever equal that adolescence of our hearts! Rapturously inhaling every breath that blows, we tried in vain to exhaust our desires; every thought was a fervour; every feeling of singular acuity. We wore out our splendid youth in the expectation of a fairer future, and the road that led to it never seemed interminable enough, however fast we strode along it, crushing on our lips those hedgerow flowers that leave in the mouth a taste of honey and an exquisite bitterness.

'Sometimes, as I passed through Paris, I would visit for a few days or a few hours, the apartment where I had spent my studious childhood; it was all silence; some absent woman's care had spread sheets over the furniture. Lamp in hand, I would go from one room to another without opening the shutters, which had been closed years before, or without pulling the curtains that were heavy with the smell of camphor. The air was close and musty. My bedroom alone was kept ready for me. In the library – the darkest and quietest of all the rooms – the books on the shelves and tables were arranged as I had left them; sometimes I would open one and sitting beside a lighted lamp, though it was daytime, happily forgot the passing hour; sometimes too I opened the grand-piano and searched my memory for some tune of bygone days; but it would come back to me in such imperfect snatches that rather than let it make me melancholy, I broke off my playing. The next day I had again left Paris far behind me.

'My heart, which was naturally loving – liquid, as it were – overflowed in all directions; no joy seemed to me exclusively my own. I invited any casual passer-by to share it, and when I was alone to enjoy my pleasure, I could only do so with the help of my pride.

'Some people taxed me with selfishness; I retorted by taxing them with stupidity. My claim was not to love anyone in particular – man or woman – but friendship itself, or affection, or love. I refused to deprive another of what I gave to one, and would only *lend* myself – just as I had no wish to appropriate another's body or heart. A nomad here too, as in nature, I took up my abode nowhere. A preference seemed to me an injustice; wishing to belong to all men, I would not give myself to any *one*.

'The memory of every town was linked in my mind to the memory of a debauch. In Venice, I took part in the masquerades. There was an evening when a concert of altos and flutes accompanied the boat in which I was love-making; it was followed by boat-loads of other young men and women. We went to the Lido in order to watch the daybreak, but before the sun rose, the music had stopped and we had fallen asleep out of weariness. But I enjoyed the very fatigue these false pleasures left behind and that sick awaking which makes us realize they have turned to dust.

'In other ports, I forgathered with the sailors of the big ships; I went down with them to the ill-lit alleys of the town; but I blamed myself for this hankering after experience – our only temptation. So leaving the sailors to their dens, I went back to the tranquil harbour; there the quiet-counselling night gave me its own interpretation of the memories I had brought away from those alleys whose strange and poignant rumours reached me through a veil of ecstasy. I preferred to all this the riches I found in the country.

'At thirty-five years old however (not wearied of travel but feeling uneasy at the excessive pride this roving life had encouraged), I realized, or persuaded myself, that I was at last ripe for some other form of existence.

' "Why, why?" I asked them, "do you speak to me of setting out again on my travels? I know that fresh flowers are blooming by all the roadsides; but it is you they are now waiting for. Bees do not go gathering honey for ever; after a time they stay at home to guard their treasure."

'I went back to the apartment I had abandoned. I uncovered the furniture; I opened the windows; and with the money I had unintentionally saved during my vagabond existence I was able to purchase all kinds of precious and fragile objects – vases, rare books and especially pictures, which my knowledge of painting enabled me to buy for practically nothing. For fifteen years I accumulated wealth like a miser; I gathered riches with all my capacities; I gathered knowledge; I learnt to play many kinds of instruments; every hour of every day was devoted to some profitable study; history and biology interested me particularly. I became acquainted with the literatures of the world, I formed many friendships which, thanks to the qualities of my heart and the unquestioned nobility of my birth, I was able to enter upon in all loyalty. They were more precious to me than all the rest, and yet not even they could hold me.

'When I was fifty, the hour having struck, I sold all my belongings, and as, with my taste and connoisseurship, I had acquired nothing which had not increased in value, in a couple of days I realized a large fortune, which I invested in such a way as to have it always at my immediate disposal. I sold absolutely everything, being determined to have no *personal* possession on this earth – not the smallest relic of the past.

'To Myrtil, the companion of my wanderings, I used to

say: "This lovely morning, this haze and this light, this breezy freshness, this pulsation of your being give you no doubt a feeling of delight. But how far greater it would be if you could abandon youself to it entirely. You imagine you are here, but the best part of you is confined elsewhere; your wife and children, your books and studies hold it prisoner and God is robbed of it.

' "Do you think that at this precise moment you can feel to the uttermost the sensation of life in all its power, completeness and immediacy, unless you forget all that is not life? The habits of your mind hamper you; you live in the past and the future, and you perceive nothing spontaneously. We only exist, Myrtil, in the *here* and *now*; in this momentariness the whole past perishes before any of the future is born. Moments! You must realize, Myrtil, the power of their *presence*. For each moment of our lives is essentially irreplaceable; you should learn to sink yourself in it utterly. If you chose, Myrtil, at this very moment, without either wife or child, you might be alone on earth in the presence of God. But you cannot forget them; and you carry with you all your past, all your loves, all the preoccupations of this earth, as if you were afraid of losing them. As for me, my whole love is available at every moment and ready for a fresh surprise; it is for ever familiar and for ever strange. You cannot imagine, Myrtil, all the forms in which God shows himself; looking too long and too passionately at one blinds you to the others. The fixity of your adoration grieves me; I should like to see it more widely diffused. God stands behind all your closed doors. All forms of God are lovable and everything is the form of God."

. . . 'When I had realized my fortune, I began by freighting a ship and went to sea with three friends, a crew of sailors and four cabin boys. I fell in love with the least beautiful of the four, but even better than his caresses – sweet as they were – I preferred gazing at the ocean. I anchored at sunset in magic harbours and left again before dawn, after I had spent the whole night sometimes, searching for love. In Venice I found a very beautiful courtesan; three nights long I loved her, for so beautiful was she, that she made me forget the delights of all my other loves. It was to her I sold or gave my boat.

'I lived for some months in a palace on the shores of Lake Como. There I gathered round me a number of the sweetest musicians, and a few beautiful women too, who could talk discreetly and well; in the evenings we would converse, while the musicians were charming us; then we would go down to the shore by a flight of marble steps, the last of which dipped in the waters of the lake; wandering boats bore us away and we lulled our loves asleep to the quiet rhythm of the oars. Drowsily we returned home; the boat started awake at the shock of landing, and Idoine, hanging on my arm, silently mounted the marble stairs.

'The year after that, I spent some time in Vendée in an immense park not far from the coast. Three poets sang the welcome I offered them in my house; they sang too the garden pools with their fishes and plants, the poplar avenues, the solitary oaks, the clumps of beeches, and the noble planning of the park. When the autumn came, I had the finest trees cut down and took pleasure in laying waste my domain. No words can describe the appearance of the park as I strolled with my guests down the paths I had allowed to become grass-grown. The blows of the wood-cutters' axes resounded from one end of the avenues to the other. The women's dresses were caught by the branches that lay across the roads. A splendid autumn blazed on the fallen trees. So glorious was the magnificence it laid upon them that for a long time I could think of nothing else – and I recognized this as a sign I was growing old.

'Since then my dwellings have been a chalet in the high Alps; a white palace in Malta, near the scented woods of Cita Vecchia where the lemons have the sharp sweetness of oranges; a travelling chaise in Dalmatia; and at the present moment, this garden on a Florentine hill (facing Fiesole) where I have gathered you together this evening.

'And you must not say I owe my happiness to circumstances; no doubt they were propitious, but I did not make use of them. Do not think that my happiness has been made with the help of riches; my heart, freed from all earthly ties, has always been poor, and I shall die easily. My happiness is made of fervour. Through the medium of all things without distinction, I have passionately worshipped.'

The monumental terrace where we were sitting (led up to by winding staircases) was lofty enough to overlook the whole town and resembled a huge ship riding at anchor over the foliage of the deep woods beneath it; at times it seemed to be really making towards the town. That summer I sometimes went up to this imaginary ship's bridge to enjoy the appeasing and contemplative quiet of evening after the turmoil of the streets. All the noises from below died away as they rose; it was as though they were waves and were breaking here. They came on and on majestically, rose and spread, widening as they struck against the walls. But I climbed higher still to where the waves could not reach. On the furthest terrace, nothing could be heard but the rustle of leaves and the wild call of the night.

Evergreen oaks and enormous laurels, planted in regular avenues, came to an end at the edge of the sky where the terrace itself ended, though here and there were rounded balustrades which jutted out still further, and made as it were balconies in the blue. There I used to sit, entranced in thought; There I imagined I was sailing in my ship. Over the dark hills that rose on the other side of the town, the sky was the colour of gold; feathery branches, starting from the terrace where I sat, drooped towards the gorgeous west, or sprang out, almost bare of leaves, into the night. There rose from the town something that looked like smoke; it was a shining, floating dust which hovered just above the places where the lights were brightest. And sometimes there shot up, as though spontaneously, into the rapture of the sultry night, a rocket let off from Heaven knows where. It would dart like a shout through the sky, quiver, turn and drop shattered, before the sound of its first mysterious explosion had died away. My favourites were those whose pale golden sparks fall so slowly and so negligently scatter, that afterwards you think that the stars too – so marvellous are they – have been born of this sudden and magical blaze, and when the sparks have disappeared, you wonder to see them still there ... until, gradually, you recognize each star fixed in its own constellation – and your rapture is increased.

'Circumstances,' said Josephus, have dealt with me in a way I cannot approve.'

'What of it?' answered Menalcas. 'I prefer to say that what is not, is what could not be.'

III

And that night it was of fruits they sang. At the gathering where Menalcas had assembled Alcides and a few others, Hylas sang

THE LAY

OF THE POMEGRANATE

> Truly, three pomegranate seeds sufficed to make Proserpina remember . . .?

You might seek long and vainly
The soul's impossible happiness.
Joys of the flesh, joys of the senses,
Let who will condemn you –
Bitter joys of flesh and senses –
Let him condemn you who will – for me, I dare not.

Truly, Didier, you eager philosopher, I admire you
If faith in your intellect gives you faith
That no joy is preferable
To the joys of the mind.
But not in all minds can such loves flourish.
And indeed, I too love the mortal tremors of my soul –
Joys of the heart, joys of the mind –
But it is you, pleasures, that I sing.

Joys of the flesh, as tender as grass,
Charming as hedge-row flowers,
Sooner faded, sooner cut down,
Than clover in the meadows,
Perishable as that heart-breaking spiraea
That sheds its flowers as soon as it is touched.

Sight! Most heart-breaking of our senses . . .
Our heart breaks at sight of what we cannot touch;
The mind can seize a thought more easily
Than the hand what our eye covets.
Oh! let your desire be for what you can touch,
Nathaniel, and seek not a more complete possession.
The sweetest joys of my senses
Have been thirsts I have quenched.

Truly, the morning mist is delicious
When the sun rises over the plains,
And delicious the sun;
Delicious the damp earth beneath our bare feet,
And the sea-soaked sand;
Delicious the water of springs to bathe in,
And to kiss, the unknown lips my lips touched in the dark . . .
But what of fruits, Nathaniel, what of fruits?

Oh! that you should not have known them!
That, Nathaniel, that is what makes me despair.
Their flesh was delicate and juicy,
Full-flavoured as raw meat,
Red as the blood that flows from a wound.
These, Nathaniel, had no need of a special thirst;
They were served in golden baskets;
Their taste was cloying at first and incredibly mawkish;
Like that of no fruit growing in any climate of ours;
It recalled the taste of over-ripe guavas;
And the sickliness of their flesh
Left a roughness in the mouth
Which could only be cured by eating another fruit;
And soon the enjoyment of them lasted
Barely longer than the moment

In which they melted in juice on the palate;
And that moment seemed all the more delightful
As the sickly taste that followed
Became all the more nauseous.
The basket was soon emptied,
And we left the last one untouched
Rather than share it.
Alas, Nathaniel, after we had eaten.
Who shall say
The bitter smart of our lips?
No water could wash them.
The longing for that fruit tormented our very souls.
Three whole days we searched the markets for it;
But the season was over.
Where, in our travels, Nathaniel,
Shall we find other fruits
To give us other longings?

*   *
      *

There are some we shall eat on terraces
Facing the sea and the setting sun.
There are some that are preserved in sweetened ice
With an added dash of liqueur.

There are some we pick from the trees
Of walled and secret gardens,
And eat in the shade during the dog-days.

Little tables will be set out;
The fruit will drop all round us
At the slightest shaking of the branches,
And the flies that drowse in them will waken.
The fallen fruit will be stored in jars,
And their scent alone would suffice to enchant us.

There are some whose peel stains the lips
And which one can only eat when one is very thirsty.
We found them by the side of shady roads;

They gleamed through a prickly foliage
Which tore our hands as we picked them —
And they barely slaked our thirst.

There are some which could be made into jam
By merely letting them bake in the sun.
There are some whose flesh always tastes sour,
Even in winter,
And a single bite of them sets the teeth on edge.

There are some whose flesh is always cold,
Even in summer.
You eat them sitting cross-legged on a mat
Inside a little inn.

And some, when they cannot be found,
Make you thirsty even to remember.

*   *
*

Nathaniel, what of pomegranates?
They were sold for a few pence in that Eastern market
Where they had been tumbled on to reed trays.
Some had rolled away into the dust
And naked children picked them up.
Their juice is tart like unripe raspberries.
Their flowers look made of wax;
They are coloured like the fruit.
Guarded treasure, honeycomb partitions,
Richness of flavour,
Pentagonal architecture.
The rind splits; the seeds fall —
Crimson seeds in azure bowls,
Or drops of gold in dishes of enamelled bronze.

Sing now the fig, Simiane,
Because its loves are hidden.

I sing the fig, said she,
Whose loves are hidden,
Whose flowering is folded away.
Closed chamber where secret nuptials are celebrated;
No perfume betrays them.
As nothing of it evaporates,
All its perfume turns to succulence and savour.
Flower without beauty; fruit of delights;
Fruit which is but the ripened flower.

I have sung the fig, said she,
Sing now of flowers.

'But,' said Hylas, 'there are fruits we have not yet sung. The poet's gift – to be thrilled by the common blackberry.'

(As for me, I care for flowers only because they are a promise of fruit.)

You have not spoken of the blackberry.

And then there is the sour sloe of country hedges,
Turned sweet by the coldness of the snow.
The medlar which can only be eaten rotten,
And the chestnut, brown as autumn leaves,
Which one puts to roast and split by the fire.

'I remember those mountain bilberries I picked one icy day in the snow.'

'I dislike the snow,' said Lothair, 'for a mystic substance which has not yet resigned itself to the earth. I hate its unfamiliar whiteness which puts a stopper on the landscape – its coldness which rejects life. I know it broods over life and protects it, but life can only be born of the snow by melting it. So that is how I want my snow – grey and dirty, half thawed and already almost turned to water for the plants.'

'Do not talk like that of snow,' said Ulrich, 'for snow too can be beautiful. It is sad and painful only when near to melting with too much love; you, who prefer love, prefer it half-melted. It is beautiful when triumphant.'

'Not for us,' said Hylas. 'And if I say *no*, it is not for you to say *yes*.'

*   *

*

And that night we each of us sang some kind of song – ballad or lay. Meliboeus sang

THE SONG

OF FAMOUS LOVERS

Zuleika! It was for your sake I refrained from drinking
The wine poured out by the cup-bearer.
At Granada I was Boabdil, and it was for you
I watered the oleanders of the Generaliffe.
I was Suleiman, Balkis, when you came from the South to prove me
with hard questions.
Tamar, I was Amnon, your brother, who pined away for vain desire
of you.
Bathsheba, when I followed a golden dove to my palace roof and saw
you going naked to the bath, I was David who sent your husband to die
for my sake.
For you, Shulamite, I sang such songs that some suppose them to be
almost sacred.
Fornarina, it was I who panted for love in your arms.
Zobeida, I am the porter you met one morning going to the market;
I was carrying an empty basket on my head, and you bade me follow
you and fill it with quinces and peaches and cucumbers of the Nile and
Egyptian limes and Sultanee citrons and spices and scents and sweets of
every kind; then, as you took a liking to me, and I complained of
fatigue, you consented to keep me for the night with your two sisters and
the three calenders, sons of kings. And we spent the night listening to
each other and telling our stories. When my turn came to tell my
story, 'Before I met you, Zobeida,' I said, 'I had no story in my life.
How should I have one now? Are not you my life?' And so saying,
the porter stuffed himself with fruit. (I remember as a small child,
dreaming of the sweetmeats of which there is so much talk in the
Arabian Nights. I have tasted some of them since then. Some were

flavoured with roses, and a friend has told me of others made with lichis.)

> *Ariadne, I am the faithless Theseus*
> *Who abandoned you to Bacchus*
> *In order to go on my way.*
>
> *Eurydice, my fair one, I am Orpheus*
> *Who in Hades repudiated you*
> *With a single glance,*
> *So irksome I felt it to be followed.*

Then Mopsus sang

THE SONG

OF REAL PROPERTY

When the rivers began to rise,
Some people took refuge in the mountains;
Some said, 'The mud will fertilize our fields';
Some said, 'It will be our ruin.'
And some said nothing at all.

When the river had risen high,
In some places trees could be seen,
In some the roofs of houses,
And steeples, and walls, and hills;
And in some nothing was to be seen at all.

Some peasants drove their herds up to the hills;
Some took their little children away in boats;
Some took away jewellery,
Eatables, papers and any money that could float;
And some took away nothing at all.
Those who had fled in boats were carried off
And woke up in countries they had never heard of.
Some woke up in America;
Some in China; some on the coast of Peru;
And some never woke up at all.

Then Guzman sang

THE LAY

OF ILLNESSES

of which I will only quote the end:

... At Damietta, I caught a fever;
At Singapore, I saw my body blossom into a lovely efflorescence of
white and mauve.
At Tierra del Fuego, all my teeth fell out.
On the Congo, a cayman devoured one of my feet.
In India, a wasting disease attacked me
And my skin turned beautifully green and as it were transparent;
And my eyes grew large and sentimental.

I lived in a luminous city; every night every crime was committed in
it and yet the galleys moored not far from the port were never full. One
morning I set sail in one of them, for the governor of the town gave me a
crew of forty rowers to use according to my fancy. Four days and four
nights we cruised; they spent their strength magnificently in my service.
The fatigue and monotony of this life quenched their turbulent spirits;
they grew weary of endlessly ploughing the ocean waves; they became
handsomer, and dreamier, as they let their memories drift away over
the wide seas. And towards evening we entered a town intersected by
canals – a town which was either gold or grey, and called Amsterdam
or Venice, according to the gloom or glow of its colour.

IV

In the gardens at the foot of Fiesole, half-way between Florence and Fiesole – in those same gardens where Pamphilio and
Fiammetta had sung in the days of Boccaccio – one evening,
when a too dazzling day had been followed by a translucent
night, we were all assembled – Simiane, Tityrus, Menalcas,
Nathaniel, Helen, Alcides and some others.

After a light repast of fruit and dainties, which we took on the terrace because of the great heat, we went down into the garden, and there, when the music was over, we wandered about under the oaks and laurels, until the time came when we could lie down on the grass beside a cool spring in the shelter of an ilex grove, and rest at ease after the heat and fatigues of the day.

I went from group to group and listened to their talk but heard only disjointed fragments, though they spoke of nothing but love.

'All pleasures are good,' said Eliphas, 'and should be tasted.'

'But not all by all,' said Tibullus. 'There must be a choice.'

A little further on. Terence was talking to Phaedrus and Bachir.

'I loved,' said he, 'a Kabyle girl; her skin was black and her flesh perfection. In the wantonest moments of pleasure – and even in its after-flagging – she kept a disconcerting gravity. She was the nuisance of my days and the delight of my nights.'

Then Simiane to Hylas:
'It is a tiny fruit that should be eaten of often.'

And Hylas sang:
There are little pleasures we have tasted that are like the sour berries one pilfers by the roadside – and one wishes they were sweeter.

We sat down on the grass beside the spring.

For a moment the song of a night-bird near by held my attention more than their talk; when I began to listen again, Hylas was saying:

... And each one of my senses has had its own desires. When I wanted to return home, I found my men and maid-servants all seated at my table. There was not the smallest place left for me. The seat of honour was occupied by Thirst; and other thirsts wanted to take the place from him. The whole table was quarrelsome, but they combined together against me. When I tried to come near the table, they were already drunk and rose against me with one accord; they turned me out of my house; they dragged me out of doors, and again I went to gather them more grapes.

73

Desires! Beautiful desires! I will bring you the juice of the grape; I will fill up your huge cups; but let me in again to my own house — so that when you fall into your drunken sleep I may once more crown myself with purple and ivy — hide the care of my brows under a garland of ivy.

Drunkenness fell upon me too and I found it difficult to go on listening; at times, when the bird stopped singing, the night seemed as silent as if I had been the only one to contemplate it; at times there seemed to spring up all round me other voices that mingled with those of my companions:

We too, we too, they said, have known the lamentable sickness of our souls.
Our desires will not let us work in peace.

. . . This summer all my desires were thirsty.
It was as though they had crossed deserts to come to me.
And I refused them drink,
So well I knew it was drinking that had made them sick.

(There were clusters of grapes in which forgetfulness lay drowsing; there were some where bees were busy feeding; there were some where the sunshine seemed to be still lingering.)
One desire comes to sit at my bedside every evening;
Every morning I find it still there.
It has watched over me all night.
I tried to weary my desire with walking;
I could only fatigue my body.

Now, Cleodalisa, sing

THE ROUNDELAY

OF ALL MY DESIRES

What did I dream of last night?
When I awoke, all my desires were thirsty,
As if they had crossed deserts while they slept.

74

To and fro, uneasily we sway
Between desire and listlessness.

Desires! Will you never weary?
Look! Oh look! Oh look! That little passing pleasure! That
pleasure that will soon have passed!
Alas! Alas! I know how to prolong my pain; but how can I entice
my pleasure to stay?

To and fro, uneasily we sway
Between desire and listlessness.

And all mankind, I thought, is like a sick man, tossing from side
to side on his bed — trying to rest, and unable even to sleep.

Our desires have already crossed many worlds;
They have never yet been glutted.
And all nature tosses
Between desire for rest and thirst for pleasure.
We have cried aloud for anguish
In deserted rooms.
We have climbed to the tops of towers
Whence only darkness was visible.
As dogs we have howled with pain
On the parching sand-hills;
As lions we have roared in the Atlas; and as camels we have
browsed on the grey weeds of the chotts and sucked the sap from hollow
reeds — for there is very little water in the desert.

As swallows we have flown across vast and barren seas;
As locusts we have laid waste whole countries in search of food.
As sea-weed the storms have rocked us;
As snowflakes we have scudded before the wind.

Oh! for an immensity of rest! I call upon salutary death, so that at
length my exhausted desire may be freed from labouring after further
metempsychoses. Desire! I have dragged you with me along the high
roads; I have denied you in the fields; I have sated you with drink in the
big towns — sated you without quenching your thirst; I have bathed you

in moonlight nights; I have taken you with me wherever I went; I have cradled you on the waves; I have lulled you to sleep on the high seas . . . Desire! Desire! What more can I do for you? What more do you want? Will you never weary?

The moon showed between the branches of the ilex-trees — monotonous, but lovely as ever. They were talking now in groups and I only heard a sentence here and there; everyone seemed to be speaking to everyone else of love, without heeding that no-one listened.

Then, as the moon disappeared behind the darkened branches of the ilex-trees, the conversation died away, and they lay quiet beside each other amongst the leaves, vaguely listening to the one or two voices that still lingered on, but more and more softly, till soon they only reached us mingled with the murmur of the stream in its mossy bed.

Simiane then rose to make herself a wreath of ivy, and I smelt the scent of the bruised leaves. Helen untwisted her hair so that it fell over her shoulders, and Rachel went to gather wet moss to press upon her eyelids and cool them to sleep.

Then even the light of the moon disappeared. I lay on the ground drowsed with enchantment and the fumes of melancholy. I did not speak of love. I waited for morning so as to be off and take again to the fortune of the road. My head had long been swimming with fatigue. I slept a few hours — then, at daybreak, I went on my way.

BOOK V

I

*Normandy, rainy, domesticated
land . . .*

'WE shall belong to each other,' you said, 'next spring, in a
certain wood I know of; I know exactly the spot, covered in
with branches and soft with moss, and what time of day it will
be, and just how mild the air; and the bird that sang there last
year will be singing there again.' But spring came late that
year; the weather was too cold, and it was a different joy that
offered.

The summer was warm and languorous – but you counted
on a woman who did not come. And you said 'Autumn at any
rate will make up for these disappointments and bring me
some consolation. She will not come, I suppose – but at any
rate the woods will redden. There will be days still warm
enough for me to go and sit beside the pond, where last year
the leaves fell so thickly. I will wait there for evening to close
in. . . . On other evenings I will go to the outskirts of the
wood, where the last rays of daylight will be lingering.' But
the autumn was rainy that year; the woods decayed without
reddening, and it was impossible to sit beside the flooded
pond.

* *
*

That year I was constantly occupied on the land. I took part
in the harvest and ploughing. I was there to witness the
approach of autumn. The season was astonishingly mild, but
rainy. Towards the end of September, a terrific gale which did
not cease blowing for twelve hours on end, withered the trees
on one side only. A little later, the leaves that had been sheltered from the wind turned golden. I was living so far out of
the world that this seemed to me as important a thing to speak
of as any other event whatever.

* *
*

There are days and then there are other days. There are mornings and evenings.

There are mornings when one gets up before daybreak, in a state of torpor. O grey autumn morning! when the soul wakes up unrefreshed, so weary and after such a burning vigil, that it longs to sleep again, prefiguring the taste of death. To-morrow I leave this shivering country; the grass is covered with hoar-frost. Like a dog which has hidden its morsels of bread and bone in the earth, against the time when it shall be hungry again, I know where to look for my little stores of pleasures – a breath of warm air at the winding of the brook; a golden lime-tree, not yet quite stripped, where the gate leads into the wood; a smile and caress for the little boy from the smithy on his way to school; further on, the smell of fallen leaves; a woman I can give a smile to; a kiss for her little child near the cottage; the sound of the smithy hammers which travels so far on an autumn morning. . . . And is that all? – Oh! to fall asleep! – It is too little – and I am too weary of hoping. . . .

*   *
*

How horrible it is to start in the semi-darkness before dawn! How one's soul and body shiver, sick and giddy! We cast one more look round to see if there is nothing else we can take away with us.

'What is it you like so much about going away, Menalcas?'
'The foretaste of death,' he answered.

No truly, what I want is not so much to see something new, as to leave behind everything that is not indispensable. Ah, Nathaniel, how many more things we might have done without! We can never strip our souls so bare as to leave enough room in them for love – love, expectation and hope – our only real possessions.

Ah! all those places where life might have been lived, where happiness would have abounded! Toiling farms, inestimable labour of the fields; fatigue; immense serenity of sleep. . . .

Away! and let there be no stopping unless it be – no matter where!

II

I left off my town clothes; they forced me to be too respectable.

*   *
*

He was there – up against me; I felt by the beating of his heart that he was a living creature, and the heat of his little body was burning. He fell asleep on my shoulder; I heard him breathing. His breath was uncomfortably warm, but I did not move for fear of waking him. His small head was jerked from side to side by the jolting of the carriage which was horribly packed with people; the others slept too, making the best of what was left of the night.

Oh yes, I have known love, and again love, and many other kinds of love; but of that tenderness I felt then, is there nothing I can say?

Oh yes, I have known love.

I have turned prowler in order to rub shoulders with all that prowls; my heart has melted with tenderness for all shelterless creatures, and I have passionately loved the vagabonds of the earth.

*   *
*

Four years ago, I remember, I spent an afternoon in this little town I am now passing through again; the season was autumn, as it is now; it was not a Sunday then either, and the heat of the day had gone by.

I walked, I remember, as I am doing now, through the streets, till I came to a terrace garden on the outskirts of the town, overlooking a stretch of beautiful country.

This is the same road I am following now and I recognize everything.

I retrace my footsteps and my emotions. . . . There was a stone bench where I sat down – there it is! I was reading. What book was it? Ah! Virgil! – And I heard the sound of the washerwoman's bats coming up to me – I hear it now. The air was calm – so it is today.

The children are coming out of school – I remember that so they were then. There are passers-by – as there were then. The sun was setting; and here is the evening; and soon the songs of daytime will be over. . . .

That is all.

'But,' said Angela, 'that's not enough to make a poem.'

'Very well,' I answered, 'let's leave it at that.'

*　　*
*

How well one knows those hurried risings before daybreak!

The postillion harnesses his horses in the yard.

Buckets of water sluice the pavement. The pump works noisily.

How one's head swims when one has been kept awake all night by thinking! This place must be left; this little room; here for a moment I laid my head; I felt; I thought; I watched. Let death come! and where it will. When life ceases, what does the *where* matter? When I was alive, it was *here*.

Quitted rooms! Never willingly have I made my marvellous departures sad. The present possession of THIS always came to me as a rapture.

So let me lean for one more moment out of *this* window. . . . The moment will come for leaving. But this one that immediately precedes it shall be mine . . . so that I may lean once more into the paling night and stretch in longing towards the infinite possibility of happiness.

Delightful moment! Shed over the blue immensity a flood of dawning light. . . .

The diligence is ready. Away! And may all I have just thought be whirled like myself into the numbing swiftness of flight! . . .

The drive through the forest. A zone of perfumed temperatures. The warmest smell is of the earth; the coolest of rotten leaves. My eyes were shut – now I open them. I was right. There are the leaves – there the freshly stirred leaf-mould. . . .

Strasbourg.

O cathedral folly,[1] with your ethereal tower! One could see from the top of the tower, as from a hovering balloon, the storks on the roofs below,

      orthodox and stiff
      with their long compass legs,

so slow, because it is so difficult to manage them.

Inns.

I slept at night in the furthest corner of the barns;
The postillion came to fetch me in the hay.

Inns.

At my third glass of kirsch, the blood began to flow more warmly under my skull;

at my fourth, I began to feel that slight intoxication which, by bringing things nearer, put them within my grasp;

At the fifth, the room in which I was, and the world itself, seemed to take on sublimer proportions, in which my sublime spirit could at last move more freely;

at the sixth, feeling slightly overcome, I fell asleep.

(All the joys of our senses have always proved as unsatisfactory as falsehoods.)

Inns.

I know the heady wine you get in inns; it has an after-taste of violets and is followed by the drugged sleep that falls upon one of an afternoon. I know those evening intoxications, when the whole world seems to rock under the weight and power of one's mind.

1. 'Sur tes ailes de pierre ô folle cathedrale!' Verlaine, *Sagesse (Translator's note.)*

Nathaniel, I will speak to you of drunkenness.

Nathaniel, often the simplest quenching of my thirst was enough to intoxicate me, I was already so drunk beforehand with desires. And what I looked for on the road first of all, was not so much an inn as my hunger.

Drunkenness of fasting, after one has walked from early dawn, when hunger, from being an appetite has turned into a dizziness. Drunkenness of thirst, after one has walked till late evening.

The most frugal repast then was as much an excess as if it had been a debauch, and the sensation of my life so intense that it was positively lyrical. At those times the voluptuous pleasure my senses brought me was such that every object that touched them became, as it were, a palpable happiness.

I know the kind of drunkenness that slightly distorts one's thoughts. I remember a day when one thought drew out of another like the tubes of a telescope; the last but one always seemed the slenderest, and then out would come one that was more fine-drawn still. I remember another day when they all became so round that really there was nothing to do but let them roll away. I remember one day when they were so elastic that each of them in turn took the shape of all the others and vice versa. And sometimes two of them ran parallel and seemed as though they were going to run on in this way to all eternity.

I know too the drunkenness that makes you think yourself better, greater, more respectable, more virtuous, richer than you are.

Autumns.

It was ploughing-time in the plains. The furrows smoked in the evening and the tired horses plodded more slowly. Every evening was as intoxicating as if I had breathed the smell of the earth for the first time. I used to enjoy going to sit on a bank on the fringe of the wood, among the dead leaves, listening to the ploughmen's songs, and watching the exhausted sun sink to sleep in the distance of the plains.

Season of mists; rainy land of Normandy. . . .

Walks. – Moorlands (without severity). – Cliffs. – Forests. – Icy brook. Rest in the shade; talks. – Russet ferns.

Ah! we thought, meadow! why did we not meet with you on our travels? What a pleasure it would have been to ride across you on horseback! (It was entirely surrounded with forests.)

Walks in the evening.

Walks at night.

Walks.

Mere *being* became an immense delight to me. I wanted to experience every form of life – that of fishes, of plants. Among all the joys of the senses, it was those of touch I envied.

A solitary tree in the autumn plain, shower enwrapped; its yellow leaves were falling; its roots, I thought, were drinking in enough water from the soaking soil to satisfy them for a very long time.

At that age, my bare feet enjoyed coming into contact with the wet earth, splashing in puddles, feeling the coolness or the warmth of the mud. I know why I was so fond of water and especially of wet things. It was because water gives us more immediately than air the sensation of varying temperature. I liked the wet breath of autumn. .... O rainy land of Normandy!

*   *

*

La Roque.

The wagons have brought home their load of scented harvest.
The barns are filled with hay.

Heavy wagons, bumping against road-side banks, jolting over ruts, how often you have brought me back from the fields, lying stretched on heaps of dry grass, among the rude haymakers!

Ah! when shall I lie stretched again upon a heap of hay and watch the evening draw in? ...

The evening was drawing in; we came to the barns – in the farmyard where the last rays of daylight were lingering.

III

THE FARM

Farmer!

Farmer, sing the farm.

Let me rest here a moment – here, near your barns, where the scent of hay will bring back to me a dream of summer.

Take your keys; one by one; open me each of your doors. . .

The first is the key of the barns. . . .

Ah! if the seasons were but trustworthy! . . . Ah! if I were but resting near your barn, in the warm hay! . . . instead of setting out, a vagabond, to conquer the arid desert by dint of fervour! . . . I should stay here and listen to the songs of the reapers; calm and confident, I should watch the harvest and its inestimable riches come home on the over-loaded wagons – like expectant answers to my questioning desires. I should no longer search for the wherewithal to satisfy them in the plains; I should stay here and gorge them at my leisure.

There is a time for laughter – and a time for laughter that is past.

There is a time for laughter, yes, – and then for the memory of laughter.

Indeed, Nathaniel, it was I, I myself who watched the stirring of this same grass – this grass which has now faded for the sake of the scented hay, as all things fade that are cut down – it was this very grass I watched, alive, green and golden, waving in the evening breeze. Ah! if the time could but return when we lay on the grassy lawns. . . .

and sheltered our love in the deep herbage of the fields.

Wild animals passed on their way under the leaves; each track was an arterial road; and when I stooped and looked at the earth close to, I saw, from leaf to leaf and flower to flower, a moving host of insects.

I used to know how damp the soil was by the vividness of the green and by the kinds of flowers that grew in it; one meadow was starred with daisies; but those we preferred, those that sheltered our love, were

86

all white with umbels, some light and feathery, others, like the great cow-parsnip, opaque and spreading. Towards evening they seemed to be floating in the deeper shadow of the grass, like gleaming medusas, free, detached from their stalks, uplifted by the rising mist.

*   *
*

The second door is the door of the granaries.

Heaps of grain, let me sing your praises! Cereals; red-gold corn; riches in expectation; inestimable stores.

Let our bread give out! Granaries, I have your key. Heaps of grain, you are there. Will you be exhausted before my hunger is appeased? Birds in the fields, rats in the granaries and all the poor at our tables. . . . Will enough be left to outlast my hunger?

Grain, I keep back a handful of you; I sow it in my fertile fields; I sow it in due season; one grain brings forth a hundredfold, another a thousandfold. . . .

Grain! if my hunger is abounding, grain! you are more abundant still!

Corn! tiny blades of green grass when first you sprout, what spikes of yellowing wealth will bow your stalks!

Golden straw, plumes and sheaves — the handful of grain I sowed . . .

*   *
*

The third door is the door of the dairy.

Peace; silence; endless dripping of the wicker trays where the cheeses are set to shrink; curds, heaped and pressed in metal moulds; on hot July days, the smell of curdled milk seemed cooler and sicklier — no, not sickly, but so mildly sour, so washed out, that it could only be smelt at the very back of one's nose, where it was already more a taste than a smell.

Churn, scoured to the utmost cleanliness. Little pats of butter lying on cabbage leaves. Red-handed dairy-maid. Windows, always kept open, but stretched with wire gauze to keep out cats and flies.

The pans are ranged in rows, full of milk which gradually turns yellow until all the cream has risen. The cream rises to the surface slowly; it puffs and wrinkles and separates from the whey. When the whey has lost all its richness, it is time to skim. . . .(But Nathaniel, I can't enter into all this. I have a friend who goes in for farming and who nevertheless can talk about it marvellously; he explains the use of everything and tells me that even the butter-milk is not wasted.) (In Normandy they give it to the pigs, but it appears there is better to be done with it than that.)

*   *
*

The fourth door opens into the cowhouse.

It is intolerably warm, but the cows smell sweet. Ah! if only I could go back to the time when the farmer's children who smelt so pleasantly of sweat used to scamper about with us in and out of the cows' legs; we searched for eggs in the corners of the hayracks; we watched the cows for hours on end; we watched the dung fall and squelch on the ground; we had bets as to which would let drop first, and one day I fled terrified, because I thought one of them was suddenly going to give birth to a calf.

*   *
*

The fifth door is the door of the fruit-house.

Bunches of grapes hang from strings in front of a sunny bay; each grape meditates and ripens, secretly ruminating light; it elaborates a perfumed sugar

Pears! Piles of apples! Fruit! I have eaten your juicy pulp. I have spat out your pips to the ground. Let them germinate there to give us fresh enjoyment!

Delicate almond; promise of wonders; little kernel; tiny spring-time that sleeps as its waits. Seed between two summers; summer-traversed seed.

Later on, Nathaniel, we will consider the pain of germination. (What an admirable effort the grass makes to shoot out from the seed!)

But for the present, let us wonder only at this — that every fecundation is accompanied by pleasure. The fruit clothes itself with flavour; and all urge towards life is enveloped with enjoyment.

Pulp of the fruit — the sapid proof of love.

*   *
*

The sixth door opens upon the cider-press.

Ah, if only I were lying in the shed — in its sultry closeness — lying beside you amidst the crushings of the apples, the crushed and acrid-smelling apples. We should try, ah! Shulamite! whether the pleasure of our bodies on the moist apples is less quick to die, longer to last, lying on the apples — sustained by their sugary smell . . .

The noise of the press lulls my memories.

*   *
*

The seventh door opens on the still.

Glooms; glowing fire; machines dimly looming in the dark; gleam of shining coppers.

Alembic; and, carefully collected, its mysterious and precious sup-puration. (Collected in this way too the resin of the pine, the morbid gums of the wild cherry, the milk of the elastic fig-tree, the wine of the pollarded palm.) Slender phial! in you is concentrated, in you spreads and breaks a whole wave of drunkenness — essence of the fruit at its sweetest and strongest, of the flower at its sweetest and balmiest.

Alembic! Ah, forming drops of beaded gold! (Some of them are more deliciously flavoured than the essential juice of cherries; others as scented as the flowering meadows.) Nathaniel! what a miraculous sight is this! The whole of spring concentrated in this little space! . . . Ah! let me flaunt it theatrically in my cups! Let me drink in this darkened room, which will soon vanish from my sight — let me drink to bestow upon my body — and to liberate my mind — the vision of all that other world I long for.

*

The eighth door is the door of the coach-house.

Ah! my golden bowl is broken – I awake. Drunkenness is never anything but a substitute for happiness. Chariots! with your help we can fly where we will; sledges, frozen lands, I harness my desires to you.

Nathaniel, we will drive to every object that exists in the world; we will reach every one in turn. I have packed my holsters with gold; in my coffers are furs that would almost make one rejoice in the cold. Wheels, who shall count your revolutions? Carriages! light-built houses, hung on springs for our comfort, let our fancies gallop away with you! Ploughs! let the oxen drag you over our fields! Dig into the earth like mattocks; the coulter that lies idle grows rusty in the shed, and all those tools . . . and you too, all our unemployed possibilities, laid by, neglected and waiting – waiting for a desire to be harnessed to you – for a traveller who longs for other, fairer countries . . .

Let our swiftness raise the powdered snow behind us! Sledges! I harness all my desires to you! . . .

*   *
*

The last door opened on to the plain.

*

BOOK VI

LYNCEUS

Zum sehen geboren,
Zum schauen bestellt.
GOETHE, *Faust*, II.

God's commandments, how you have hurt my soul!
  God's commandments, are there ten of you or twenty?
  How much narrower still are your limits to become?
  Will you go on forbidding me more and still more?
  Does the thirst for all I have found beautiful on earth condemn me
to still further chastisements?
  God's commandments, you have injured my soul,
  You have set walls round the only waters that could slake my thirst.

  . . . But now, Nathaniel, I am full of pity
  for the delicate sins of men.

*   *
*

Nathaniel, I will teach you that there is nothing that is not divinely natural.

Nathaniel, I will speak to you of everything.

I will put a crook in your hands, little shepherd, and, over hill and dale, we will gently guide our sheep, which have never yet followed any master.

Shepherd, I will guide your desires to all that is beautiful on earth.

Nathaniel, I will inflame your lips with a new thirst, and then I will put to them cups of a cooling drink. I have drunk of them. I know the springs where hot lips can quench their thirst.

Nathaniel, I will speak to you of springs.

There are springs that gush forth from rocks;
There are some that well up under glaciers;
There are some so blue that they look deeper than they are.
(At Syracuse, this is why the Cyane is so wonderful.

Azure source; sheltered pool; water blossoming into papyrus; we bent over the boat's side; over a ground that looked made of sapphires, azure fish were swimming.

At Zaghouan are the springs of the Nymphaea that watered Carthage of old.

At Vaucluse, the water gushes from the earth as abundantly as if it had been flowing for a long time; it is already almost a river, and you can follow it up stream underground; it flows through caverns and becomes imbued with darkness. The torch-lights flicker and grow dim; then you get to a place so dark that you think – no, impossible to go up any further.)

There are ferruginous springs that give a gorgeous colouring to the rocks.

There are sulphurous springs whose green, warm waters at first look poisonous; but, Nathaniel, when people bathe in them their skin becomes so exquisitely soft that it feels more delicious than ever to the touch.

There are springs from which mists rise in the evening – mists which float round them all night, and in the morning slowly dissipate.

Little, simple springs, that dwindle away to nothing among reeds and moss.

Springs where washerwomen come to wash their clothes and which turn mill-wheels.

Inexhaustible supply! up-leaping fountains! Below the springs what abundance of waters, what hidden reservoirs, what unsealed wells! The hardest rocks will be riven. The mountain-side will be clothed with green; waste lands will rejoice and all the bitterness of the desert will flower.

More springs gush from the earth than we have thirsts with which to drink them.

Waters ceaselessly renewed; celestial vapours dropping and re-dropping.

If there is a dearth of water in the plains, let the plains come to drink at the mountains – or let the subterranean channels carry the water of the hills to the plains. Granada's prodigious irrigation. Reservoirs; Nymphaea. Indeed, there is extraordinary beauty in springs – extraordinary delight in bathing in them. Pools! Pools! we shall step out of you purified.

As the sun in the light of dawn,
As the moon in the dews of night.
So, in your running moisture
We will lave our weary limbs.

There is extraordinary beauty in springs; and in waters that filter underground. They come up as clear as if they had flowed through crystal; there is extraordinary delight in drinking them; they are as pale as air, as colourless as if they were non-existent, and as tasteless; one only becomes aware of them by their excessive coolness, and that is the secret of their virtue. Can you understand, Nathaniel, that it is tempting to drink of them?

The greatest joys of my senses
Have been the thirsts I have quenched.

Now, Nathaniel, you shall hear

THE LAY

OF MY QUENCHED THIRSTS

For we have stretched our lips towards brimming cups
More eagerly than towards kisses;
Brimming cups, so soon emptied.

The greatest joys of my senses
Have been the thirsts I have quenched.

*

There are drinks which are prepared
With the juice of squeezed oranges,
*   Or lemons, or limes —*
Refreshing drinks, because they taste
Both sweet and sour.

I have drunk out of glasses so thin
That your mouth was afraid of breaking them

Before ever your teeth touched them;
And drink seems to taste better in them
Because there is almost nothing between your lips and it.
I have drunk out of elastic bowls
Which you squeezed with both hands
To make the wine rise to your lips.
I have drunk thick syrups out of coarse inn glasses
After days spent walking in the sun;
And sometimes after the icy water of a cistern
I have better enjoyed the evening shade.
I have drunk water that had been kept in skins,
And that smelt of tarred goat-hide.

I have drunk water as I lay stretched on the banks
Of streams where I wanted to bathe,
While my two bare arms plunged into the running water
Until they touched the bottom,
Where white pebbles can be seen stirring . . .
And the cool soaked into me by the shoulders too.

The shepherds drank water out of their hands;
I taught them to suck it up through straws.
There were days when I walked in the blazing sun,
During the hottest hours of the summer day,
In search of a fiercer thirst to quench.

And do you remember, my friend, that once, during that frightful
journey of ours, we got up in the middle of the night, perspiring, to
drink out of the earthenware jar which had made the water icy?

Cisterns, hidden wells, to which the women go down.
Waters which have never seen the light; which taste of darkness.
Waters which are bubbling with air.
Waters which are abnormally transparent; which I should have pre-
ferred blue — or rather green — so that they would have seemed icier —
with a slight taste of aniseed.

The greatest joys of my senses
Have been the thirsts I have quenched.

No! I have not yet counted all the stars of the sky, all the pearls of the sea, all the white feathers strewn on the shores of gull-haunted bays.

Nor all the whispering of the leaves, nor all the smiles of dawn, nor all the laughter of summer. And now, what more shall I say? Because my lips are silent, do you think my heart is still?

> O meadows steeped in azure!
> O meadows soaked in honey!

Bees will come, laden with wax . . .

I have seen dark ports at night where the dawn lay hidden behind a trellis of yards and sails; I have seen boats steal off in the morning between the hulls of the big ships. One had to stoop one's head as one passed under their cables and moorings.

At night, I have seen galleons in countless numbers thrust out into the night, thrust out towards the day.

*   *
*

They do not gleam like pearls, they do not shine like water, and yet the pebbles in the path are bright. In the trellised path where I was walking, how gently the light was captured!

But ah! Nathaniel, what can I say of phosphorescence? Matter is infinitely permeable by mind, submissive to all laws, obedient, transparent through and through. Did we not see the walls of the Mahometan city redden in the evening and faintly glimmer at night? Walls, into whose deep recesses light streamed all day long, metal-white walls, where at noon treasures of light are accumulated – at night, they seemed to be repeating it – very faintly telling it over. Cities! You looked to me transparent! Lying below me, as I stood gazing down on you from the hill, you shone in the deep shadow of the enveloping night like those hollow alabaster lamps – symbol of a pious heart, because they are filled with brightness and seem porous to the light that streams from them like milk.

White pebbles of the shady path – receptacles of brightness.

White heather in moorland twilights; marble pavements of the mosques; anemones flowering in sea grottoes. . . . All whiteness is stored light.

I learnt to judge all creatures by their receptivity of light; some which absorbed the sun during the daytime, at night looked to me like cells of brightness.

I have seen a river running at midday through the plains and further on gliding at the foot of black, impenetrable rocks. It was there that it poured out its glittering treasures of gathered gold.

But, Nathaniel, here I will speak to you only of *things* – not of

THE INVISIBLE REALITY – for

. . . as the most wonderous sea-weed grows lustreless when it is taken out of the water,

so . . . etc.

The landscape's infinite variety continually proved to us that we had not yet tasted all the forms of happiness, meditation or melancholy that it possibly contained. I know that on certain days of my childhood, when I was still subject to sadness, there were moments on the moor in Brittany when it would suddenly fly from me and take refuge in the landscape which seemed to me full of sympathy and understanding. And so it was outside me that I could look at my sadness, with a delicious sense of ease.

Perpetual novelty.

He does something very simple and then says, 'I realized that that particular thing had never been done, or thought, or said before.'

And suddenly everything struck me as possessing perfect virginity. (The whole past of the world completely absorbed in the present moment.)

* *
*

Rising. God must not be kept waiting, I cried as I washed; however early one gets up, there are always living things already astir; earlier to bed than we, they do not keep Him waiting so long.

> *Dawns, you were our dearest delights!*
> *Springtime, dawn of the summer!*
> *Dawn, springtime of the day!*
> *We were not yet up*
> *When the rainbows appeared . . .*
> *. . . never early enough in the morning,*
> *Or, may-be, never late enough at night*
> *To catch the moon . . .*

Siestas.

I have known the mid-day sleep of summer – the sleep that follows work begun too early in the morning – overpowering sleep.

2 o'clock. The children are resting in bed. The silence is stifling. One might play the piano a little? I won't. Smell of chintz curtains. Hyacinths and tulips. Linen-room.

5 o'clock. Waking bathed in perspiration; a beating heart, a shuddering body, a light brain; flesh available for any call – porous flesh, too deliciously open to invasion from the outside. A low sun; yellow lawns; eyes that open at the close of day. O luscious wine of evening thoughts! O unfurling of evening flowers! Now to bathe one's forehead in warm water; to go out. . . . Espaliers; walled gardens in the sun. The road; cattle returning from their pastures; sunset – why trouble to look at it? Enough of admiration.

Now to go in. To begin work again beside the lamp.

*   *
*

What of sleeping places, Nathaniel?

I have slept on haystacks; I have slept in the furrows of cornfields; I have slept on the grass in the sun; in haylofts at night; I have slung my hammock between trees; I have been rocked asleep by the waves, lying on the ship's deck or in a narrow berth opposite the port-hole's glassy eye. There were beds where courtesans awaited me; and others where I awaited young boys. There were some upholstered with stuffs so soft that they seemed, like my body, to be designed as instruments of love. I have slept in camps on plank beds where sleep was like annihilation. I have slept in railway carriages, without losing for a second the sensation of motion.

Nathaniel, there are wonderful preludes to sleep; there are wonderful awakings from it; but there is no wonderful sleep, and I only care for a dream in so far as I believe it a reality. For the best sleep is not worth

the moment of awaking.

I acquired the habit of sleeping by a wide open window, almost directly under the sky. On hot July nights, I have slept completely stripped in the moonlight; the blackbirds woke me up at dawn; I dipped into cold water and prided myself on beginning the day very early. In the Jura, my window opened on to a little valley which very soon filled up with snow; from my bed I could see the outskirts of a wood where crows were flying, or rooks; early in the morning the cow-bells woke me up; near my lodging was the fountain where the cow-herds came to water their cattle. I remember it all.

In the inns of Brittany, I liked the contact of the rough sheets smelling sweet of the laundry. At Belle-Isle, the singing of the sailors woke me up; I ran to the window and saw the boats sailing away; then I went down to the sea.

Some dwellings are marvellous. I never wanted to stay long in any of them. I was in constant fear of doors that shut – traps – cells that close down over the mind. The nomad's life is the shepherd's. (Nathaniel, I will put my crook in your hand and you, in your turn, shall tend my sheep. I am tired. It is for you now to start on your way; all the countries of the world lie open before you and the unsatisfied flocks bleat continually after fresh pastures.)

Nathaniel, I was sometimes detained by the strangest lodgings. There were some in the middle of forests; some on the water's edge; some that were very spacious. But as soon as familiarity made me cease to notice them, as soon as I was no longer astonished by them, no longer drawn by the promise of their windows, and was on the verge of beginning to think, I left them.

(I can hardly explain to you, Nathaniel, this exasperated desire I had for novelty; not that I felt as if I had skimmed the cream off things, or deflowered them; but my first sudden sensation was so intense that no further repetition could increase it; so that if it often happened to me to return to the same town and the same places, it was in order to feel in them a change of hour or season, which was more noticeable when the outlines were familiar; and if, when I was staying at Algiers, I spent the end of every day in the same little Moorish café, it was to observe the imperceptible change in each individual, from one evening to the next, to watch time modifying – slowly modifying – the same tiny bit of space.)

In Rome, where I lived in a room near the Pincio on a level with the street, the flower-sellers would come to my window (it had bars like a prison) to offer me their roses; the air was fragrant with them. In Florence, I could see the yellow Arno in flood without rising from my table. At Biskra, Meriem came to my terrace by moonlight in the vast silence of the night. She was wrapped in a big tattered white haik which she dropped laughing at the threshold of my glazed door; in my room a feast of dainties awaited her. At Granada, my mantel-piece had two water-melons on it instead of candlesticks. At Seville, there are *patios* – pale marble courts, full of shade and cool water – running, streaming water which makes a sound of lapping in a basin in the middle of the court.

A wall, stout against the North wind and porous to the southern sun; a house on wheels, a travelling house, transparent to all the blessings of the South. . . . What does a room mean for us, Nathaniel? A shelter in a landscape.

*   *
*

I will speak to you of windows too; at Naples, there were talks on the balconies, and evening reveries beside the light dresses of the women; half-drawn curtains separated us from the noisy company in the ball-room. Such delicately heart-broken words were exchanged that after them one stayed for a little without speaking; then there rose up from the garden the overpowering smell of the orange-blossom and the song of the summer nightbirds; then, at moments the birds themselves fell silent and one heard, faintly – very faintly – the sound of the waves.

Balconies; bowers of wistaria and roses; repose of evening; balmy airs.

(This evening a melancholy gale is wailing and weeping against my window-panes; I am trying to prefer it to anything else.)

* *
*

Nathaniel, I will speak to you of towns.

I have seen Smyrna lying like a little girl asleep on the shore; Naples like a wanton bathing in the sea, and Zaghouan like a Kabyle shepherd whose cheeks the coming of dawn has crimsoned. Algiers trembles for love in the sun, and swoons for love at night.

In the North I have seen villages slumbering in the moon-light; the walls of the houses were alternately blue and yellow; round them stretched the plain; the fields were littered with huge haystacks. You go out when the country is deserted; the village is asleep when you come in.

* *
*

There are towns and towns; sometimes it is impossible to guess why they have been built in that particular place. Oh! towns of the East, of the South; towns with flat roofs and white terraces where foolish women come to dream at night. Pleasures; love-feasts; squares lighted by tall lamps which, seen from the neighbouring hills, look like a phosphorescence in the night.

Eastern towns! alight with revelry; streets called '*holy streets*', in which the cafés are full of courtesans who are excited to dance by the over-shrillness of the music; white-robed Arabs flit about, and young boys – too young (weren't they?) to be acquainted with love. (There were some whose lips were hotter than little unfledged birds.)

Northern towns! Wharves and docks; factories; towns whose smoke hides the sky. Fine buildings; towering cranes; presumptuous arches. Processions cavalcading through the broad streets; eager crowds. Asphalt gleaming after the rain; boulevards where the chestnut-trees languish; women who are always lying in wait for you. There were nights – nights so utterly enervating – that the slightest solicitation would have made me faint.

11 *p.m.* Closing time; the strident noise of iron shutters. Cities. At night as I passed through the deserted streets, the rats were scuttling back to their drains. Through the cellar lights I could see half naked men at work baking bread.

*   *
*

O cafés! where we sat up like lunatics till all hours of the night; the excitement of drink and talk finally got the better of sleepiness. Cafés! Some were luxurious, full of paintings and mirrors and frequented only by persons of extreme elegance! Others were small; people sang comic songs in them and the women pulled their skirts up very high to dance!

In Italy, there were some which overflowed on to the piazzas on summer evenings and in which they gave you very good lemon ices. In Algeria, there was one where they smoked kief and where I very nearly got myself assassinated; the next year it was shut up by the police, for it was the haunt of suspicious characters.

Still more cafés . . . O Moorish cafés! Sometimes you find in them a poet story-teller who tells a long, long story; how many nights I went to listen to him, without understanding a word! . . . But more than all the rest, without hesitation, it is you I prefer, little café of Bab-el-Derb – place where silence gathers and days end; clay-built hut on the very edge of the Oasis, with nothing but desert stretching beyond it. There, after the hot day had panted itself out, I watched the more peaceful night descending. Beside me sang the monotonous ecstasy of a flute.

And I think of you too, little café of Shiraz – tavern which Hafiz sang; Hafiz, drunk with love and the cupbearer's wine, silent on the terrace where the roses have climbed up to him, Hafiz, who beside the sleeping cupbearer, awaits as he writes his verses – all night long awaits the coming day.

(I wish I could have been born at a time when a poet would have had only to name a thing in order to sing it. On each thing in turn my admiration would have alighted, and my praise would have been the proof of its existence – its all-sufficient reason.)

*   *
*

Nathaniel, we have not yet looked at leaves together. All the curves of leaves . . .

Foliage; green grottoes, riddled with light; backgrounds that shift with the slightest breeze; swayings; shapes that eddy; fretted outlines; elastic-jointed boughs; flexuous swingings; lamellated, honeycombed . . .

Boughs that are unequally stirred because the elasticity of their twigs is diverse, which makes their resistance to the wind diverse, and diverse too the impulsion it gives them . . . etc. Now let's go on to something else. To what? – Since we neglect composition, we should neglect choice too. . . . Available, Nathaniel, available!

. . . and by the sudden and *simultaneous* straining of all our senses, succeed in making of our sense of life itself (difficult to explain this) the concentrated sensation of every impact from the outside . . . (or vice versa). Here I am; here, in this hollow in the ground, and there sinks

into my ears: this incessant noise of water; the noise of this
wind in these pine-trees – louder and then less
loud; this intermittent noise of grasshoppers,
etc.

into my eyes: this brightness of sun in the stream; the stirring
of these pine-branches ... (Hullo! a squirrel!)
... my foot digging a hole in this moss, etc.

into my flesh: the sensation of this dampness, of this softness of
the moss (oh! what thorn is that pricking me?
...); of my head in my hand; of my hand on
my head, etc.

in my nostrils: ... (hush! here comes the squirrel), etc.

And all this *together*, in a little packet – *that* is life. *Only* that?
No! there is always something else besides.

Do you think then that I am nothing but a rendez-vous of
sensations? My life is always THAT, plus myself. Another
time I will speak to you about *myself*. And today you shall not
hear either

THE LAY

OF THE DIFFERENT FORMS OF THE SPIRIT

nor

THE LAY

OF BEST FRIENDS

nor

THE BALLAD

OF ALL ENCOUNTERS

in which these phrases occurred among others:

*At Lecco, on the Lake of Como, the grapes were ripe. I climbed to
the top of an enormous hill where there were ruined walls of ancient
castles. The smell of grapes was so cloying that it nearly made me sick;
it penetrated like a taste to the back of my nostrils, so that there was
no further surprise when afterwards I ate them – but it was so thirsty
and so hungry that two or three bunches were enough to make me
drunk.*

. . . But in this Ballad it was especially of men and women that I spoke, and I am not telling it to you now because in this book I have resolved to put no personalities. Have you noticed that in this book there is *no one*? And even I myself am nothing in it but Vision. Nathaniel, I am Lynceus, the keeper of the tower. Long enough the night had lasted. From the top of the tower I called to you so impatiently, dawns! Never radiant enough dawns!

Till the night was drawing to an end I clung to the hope of a new light. I cannot see it yet, but I hope; I know in which quarter the day will break.

Yes, a whole people is getting ready; from the top of the tower I hear a rumour in the streets. The day will break! The people, rejoicing, are already on the march to meet the sun.

'What of the night, watchman, what of the night?'

'I see a generation coming up and I see a generation going down. I see a vast generation coming up, coming up to life, all armed, all armed with joy.'

What do you see from the top of your tower? What do you see, Lynceus, my brother?

Alas! Alas! Let the other prophet lament. The night comes and so does the day.

Their night comes and so does our day. Let him sleep who will. Lynceus! Come down from your tower now. The day is breaking. Come down into the plain. Look more closely now, more carefully. Come, Lynceus, come nearer. This is the day and we believe in it.

BOOK VII

Quid tum si fuscus Amyntas.

VIRGIL.

DEPARTURE from Marseilles in a violent wind.

A magnificent day. Unseasonably warm.

Rocking of the masts. A glorious, white-crested sea and wave-whipped boat. A triumphant impression of glory. The recollection of all past departures.

Sea passage.

How often I have watched for the dawn ...
    ... on a desperate sea ...
        and the dawn came without calming the sea.
Perspiring temples. Qualms. Faintness. Sinkings.

Night at Sea.

Relentless sea. Rushing of water on the deck. Throbbing of the screw ...

O deadly perspiration!

A pillow for my splitting head ...

This evening the moon shone, full and splendid, on the deck – and I was not there to see it.

Dread of the next wave. Sudden breaking of the mass of water; suffocation; risings; fallings. Helplessness; what am I? A cork – a wretched cork on the waters.

Oh, to abandon oneself to the oblivion of the waves! To enjoy the luxury of renouncement! To become a thing!

End of the night.

In the excessive chilliness of the morning, the deck is being washed with sea-water drawn up in buckets. All-pervading draughts. In my cabin I hear the noise of scrubbing-brushes on the boards. Great thudding shocks. I tried to open my porthole. Too strong a gust of sea-air blew on my dank temples. I tried to shut it again ... My berth! To fall upon it! Ah! what horrible pitchings outside the harbour! Whirligig of reflections and shadows on the wall of my white cabin – my tiny cabin!

My eye wearied with seeing ...

I suck up this iced lemonade through a straw ...

To wake up after it all in a new country, as after a convalescence. ... Unimagined strangeness.

*   *
*

To wake up one morning on a beach;
All night to have been cradled by the waves.

Algiers.

Plateaux where the low hills fall to rest;
Sunsets where days vanish in the west;
Beaches where the seascape breaks in lines;
Nights in which love fades away in sleep ...
The night will come towards us, a vast haven;
Thoughts and rays and melancholy birds
Will come to rest there from the light of day;
In thickets where the shadows are at peace ...
And the calm meadow-waters and the weedy springs.

... Then, when at home again, after voyaging,
The calm of shores – ships riding in the port.
On waves that have grown peaceful we shall see
The migrant bird asleep and the boat moored.
The coming night opens us its vast haven
Of silence and of love.
This is the hour of sleep.

March, 1895.

Blidah! Flower of the Sahel! In winter, faded and unlovely, in the spring I thought you beautiful. It was a rainy morning;

the sky was indolent, gentle and sad; the scent of the flowering trees floated hither and thither in your long alleys. A fountain played in your quiet pool; the barrack bugles sounded in the distance.

This is now the other garden – a forsaken wood where the white mosque glimmers faintly in the olive trees. Sacred wood! My mind, infinitely weary, and my flesh, exhausted by love's restlessness, come here this morning to rest. The sight of you last winter had left me with no presentiment, creepers, of your marvellous blooming. Violet wistaria swaying among the branches, clusters like drooping censers, and petals fallen on the golden sand of the paths. Sounds of water; liquid sounds of lapping on the pool's edge; giant olive-trees, white spiraea, bowers of lilac, tufts of thorn, bushes of roses. To come here alone and to think of winter and to feel so weary that even spring, alas! brings with it no surprise; and even to wish for greater austerity; for such smiling loveliness, alas! is but a mocking invitation to him who walks here alone in empty alleys, peopled only with troops of obsequious desires. And notwithstanding the noise of waters in the quiet pool, all around, the attentive silence is full – only too full – of absence.

*   *
*

I know the spring where I shall go
To cool my burning eyes.
The sacred wood; I know the way,
The leaves, the cool of its green glade;
I shall go there at night when all is still,
And the soft air invites us more to sleep than love.
Cold spring, into whose depths
The whole dark night will sink!
Iced water, where the transparent morn
Will re-appear, shivering and white! Fountain of purity!
Shall I not find once more in the coming dawn
The charm it had when I could still behold with wonder
Daylight and all the world of things?
When I go there to cool my burning eyes.

You cannot imagine, Nathaniel, the effect produced by this saturation of light, and the sensual ecstasy that comes from this persistent heat. ... An olive-branch in the sky; the sky above the hills; the song of a flute at a café door ... Algiers was so hot, so full of rejoicings, that I determined to leave it for two or three days; but at Blidah, where I took refuge, I found the orange-trees in flower ...

I go out as soon as it is morning; I walk; I look at nothing and see everything; a marvellous symphony of subconscious sensations is formed and harmonized within me. Time passes; my excitement abates, like the sun's course, which becomes slower as it becomes more vertical. Then I choose something – a creature or a thing – to fall in love with. But it must be something moving, for directly my emotion becomes fixed, it ceases to be vital. I feel then, at every fresh moment, that I have never before seen, never before tasted anything. I follow madly in a wild pursuit the things that fly and escape me. Yesterday, I ran up to the top of the hills that look down upon Blidah, in order to keep the sun in sight a moment longer; in order to see the sun set and the clouds shed their glow on to the white terraces. I surprise shade and silence under the trees; I roam furtively in the light of the moon; I often have the sensation of swimming, the warm luminous air enwraps and uplifts me so gently.

... I believe the path I follow is *my* path and that I follow it as I should. A vast confidence has become habitual to me which would be called faith, if it had subscribed to any vows

Biskra.

There were women waiting on the doorsteps; behind them a staircase mounted steeply. They sat there on their doorsteps, grave, painted like idols, crowned with diadems of coins. At night the streets became animated. There were lamps burning at the top of the staircases, and in each niche of light made by the well of the staircase sat a woman; their faces were in the shadow beneath the gleaming gold of their diadems; each woman seemed to be waiting for me – for me in particular; in order to go upstairs, you added a gold coin to the diadem; the courtesan as she passed put out the lamps; you went into her small room, drank coffee out of little cups and then fornicated on a kind of low divan.

*   *
*

Biskra Gardens.

You wrote to me, Athman: 'I tend my flocks under the palm-trees. The palm-trees are expecting you. You will come back! Spring will be in the branches; we shall walk about together and have no more thoughts . . .'

You will spend no more time, Athman, expecting me under the palm-trees and watching for the spring. I have come; the spring is in the branches; we walk about together and have no more thoughts.

Biskra Gardens.

Grey weather today; warm and damp; sweet scented mimosas. Thick drops, large, floating drops form, as it were, in the air . . . They are stopped by the leaves, weigh them down and then fall suddenly to the ground.

. . . I remember the rain one summer's day – but were those warm drops really rain? – those large heavy drops that fell on a palm-garden suffused in a green and rosy light. Drops so weighty that leaves and blossoms and branches rolled down with them and lay scattered on the water like a lavish love-gift of loosened garlands. The streams bore off the pollen for distant fertilizations; their waters were yellow and troubled. The fish gasped in the pools. On the surface of the water one could hear the snapping of the carps' mouths.

Before the rain came down, the rattling breath of the South wind had struck its scorching deep into the earth, and then rising vapours filled the paths under the branches; the mimosas drooped their boughs as though to shelter the joyous company on the benches. It was a garden of delights; and the men in their woollen draperies and the women in their striped haiks waited for the damp to soak into them. They remained sitting as before on the benches, but every voice grew silent as they listened to the falling drops and let the brief midsummer shower weigh down their clothes with its water and drench them to the skin. The warm moisture of the air, the richness of the foliage were such that I too, remained sitting on the bench beside the others powerless to resist love. – And then, when the rain had stopped and only the branches were left dripping, they all took off their shoes and sandals, and paddled in the wet earth's delicious softness with their bare feet.

*   *
*

A garden where no one ever goes; two young boys dressed in white woollen garments took me to it. A very long garden with a gate at the further end. The trees are taller here; the sky lower – the sky is entangled in the trees. Walls. Whole villages in the rain. And in the distance, mountains; streams forming; trees feeding; solemn, swooning fecundations; wandering perfumes.

Covered-over rivulets; channels (a mingling of leaves and blossoms) called *seghias* because their waters flow slowly.

The Gafsa swimming-pool with its dangerous charms – ('*Nocet cantantibus umbra*'). The night now is cloudless, profound, with the faintest veil of mist.

(One beautiful boy, dressed in Arab style in a garment of white wool, was called '*Azous*', which means *Beloved*. Another was called '*Ouardi*', which means that he was born in the time of roses.)

> *And waters warm and soft as air,*
> *In which our lips have dipped . . .*

Dark water, which we could hardly see in the night – until the moon silvered it. It seemed to come to life among the leaves, and there were night creatures stirring in it.

*   *
*

To spring up at daybreak – up and out into the renovated air.
An oleander branch will quiver in the shivering dawn.

In this tree there were birds singing. They sang, oh! louder
than I thought it possible for birds to sing. It was as if the tree
itself were singing – shouting with all its leaves – for the birds
could not be seen. They will die of it, I thought; their passion
is too great; but what possesses them this evening? Don't they
know that after the night there will be another morning? Are
they afraid they will sleep for ever? Do they want to wear
themselves out with love in a single evening? Do they think
they will be condemned for ever after to a night of infinite
length? Short night of late spring! Ah! what joy that the
summer dawn will wake them, and so thoroughly, that they
will only just remember enough of their sleep to make them
next evening a little less afraid of dying.

The bushes are silent; but the desert all round vibrates with
the locusts' love-song.

*   *
*

The days are drawing out. To lie down here, out of doors. The
fig-leaves have grown broader; they scent the hands that crush
them; their stalks weep milk.

The heat is growing fiercer. Ah! here comes my flock of
goats; I hear the flute of the goat-herd I love. Will he come to
me? Or shall *I* go to meet him?

The hours pass slowly. A last year's pomegranate is still
hanging from the tree; it is split open and dried up; on the

same branch the buds of fresh blossoms are already swelling. Turtledoves are flying among the palms. The bees are busy in the meadow.

(I remember a well near Enfida with beautiful women going down to it; near by was an immense rock, grey and pink; its summit, I was told, was haunted by bees; yes, tribes of murmurous bees; they make their hives in the rock. When summer comes, the hives burst with heat and let their honey trickle down the face of the rock; the men of Enfida go and collect it.) Goatherd, come! (I am chewing a fig-leaf.)

Summer! golden ooze; profusion; glory of increased light; immense overflowing of love! Who wants to taste honey? The waxen cells have melted.

And the most beautiful thing I saw that day was a flock of sheep being driven home to their pen. Their little feet, hurrying along sounded like the pattering of a shower; the sun was setting in the desert and they raised a cloud of dust.

* *
*

Oases! They floated in the desert like islands; the green of the distant palm-trees gave promise of the spring that fed their roots. Sometimes it rose abundant and oleanders bent over it. On that particular day, we arrived there at about ten o'clock, and I refused at first to go any further; the charm of those gardens and their flowers was so great that I wanted never to leave them. Oases! (Ahmet told me that the next one was lovelier still.)

Oases! The next one was lovelier still, fuller of flowers and murmurs. Taller trees bent over more abundant waters. It was noon. We bathed. Then we had to leave that too.

Oases! What shall I say of the next? It was lovelier still and we stayed there till evening.

Gardens! Nevertheless I will repeat again how hushed and delicious your quiet was at the fall of evening. Gardens! There were some in which one seemed to wash; some which were just monotonous orchards of ripening apricots; others were full of bees and flowers, and the scents that floated in them were so strong that they might have served for food and went to our heads like liqueurs.

The next day I cared for nothing but the desert.

Oumach.

Then there was that oasis set in the rock and sand; we reached it at noon, and in such blazing heat that the village seemed too exhausted to notice us. The palm-trees did not bend; the old men sat gossiping in the doorways; the grown men had fallen asleep; the children were chattering at school; the women were nowhere to be seen.

Streets of that earth-built village, pink by day and violet at sunset; you are deserted at noon, but you will come to life in the evening; then the cafés will fill up, the children come out of school, the old men still sit gossiping on their thresholds, the last rays of the sun fall asleep, and the women go up to their house-tops and, unveiled like flowers, talk endlessly of the tedium of their existence.

That street in Algiers was pervaded at noon by a smell of aniseed and absinthe. In the Moorish cafés of Biskra, they drank nothing but coffee, lemonade or tea – Arab tea, sweet and peppery like ginger; a drink that evoked an even more exaggerated – an even further East. Too sickly; impossible to finish the cup.

In the Touggourt market-place there were vendors of aromatics. We bought different kinds of resins from them. Some were meant to smell, some to chew, some to burn. Those meant to burn were generally in the shape of pastilles; when lighted, they gave out a quantity of acrid smoke mixed with some sort of very subtle perfume; their smoke helps to excite religious fervour and is used in the mosque ceremonies. Those meant to chew filled one's mouth with a bitter taste and stuck disagreeably to one's teeth; the taste lasted long after one had spat them out. Those meant to smell simply smelt.

At the marabout of Temassine's, scented cakes were served us at the end of the meal. They were decorated with gold, or grey, or pink leaves and seemed to be made of kneaded bread-crumbs. They crumbled in one's mouth like sand; but I thought them not unpleasant. Some of them smelt of roses, others of pomegranates; others had completely lost all their scent. At these meals it was impossible to get drunk except by smoking. A tedious number of dishes were handed round and the conversation changed with every fresh course. Then a Negro poured some aromatic water out of a ewer on to your fingers. The water fell into a basin. In the same way the women of those countries wash one after love-making.

Touggourt.

Arabs encamped in the market-place; fires are lighted – their smoke barely visible in the evening.

Caravans! Caravans arriving in the evening; caravans gone before morning; horribly wearied, mirage-bewildered cara-vans, and now at last given up to despair! Caravans! Would that I too might go with you, caravans!

Some were going East to fetch sandalwood and pearls, honeycakes from Bagdad, ivories, embroideries.

Some were going South to fetch amber and musk, gold dust and ostrich feathers.

And some, going West, started in the evening and were lost to sight in the sun's last dazzling effulgence.

I saw the harassed caravans returning; the camels knelt down in the market-place and were at last freed from their burdens – bundles done up in coarse canvas, the contents of which it was impossible to guess at. Other camels were carry-ing women hidden in a sort of palanquin. Others carried the material for the tents which were set up for the night. Oh, the splendour, the immensity of such fatigue in the boundless desert! – Fires are lighted on the market-places for the evening meal.

★ ★
★

How often, ah! risen at daybreak, with eyes turned towards the crimson East, streaming with more rays than a glory, how often, at the edge of the oasis, where the last palm-trees dwindle away, and life no longer triumphs over the desert – how often, as though irresistibly drawn towards that fountain of radiance, too dazzling already for human eyes to bear, have I yearned for that vast light-flooded, heat-scorched plain! . . . What transport of ecstasy, what violence of love will ever be ardent enough to vanquish the ardour of the desert?

Harsh land; unsmiling, ungentle land; land of passion and of fervour; land beloved of the prophets – ah! sorrow stricken, glorious desert, I have passionately loved you.

I have sometimes seen the white crust of salt on the mirage-haunted chotts take on the appearance of water. That the azure of the sky should be reflected in those shimmering sea-blue chotts is comprehensible enough – but why do tufts of reeds and crumbling, schistous cliffs, become floating visions of barks, distant visions of palaces? And all those distortions seem suspended over imaginary depths of water! (On the borders of the chott – a horrible kind of burning marl mixed with salt – the smell was nauseous.)

I have seen the mountains of Amar Khadou under the slanting rays of the early sun turn rose-colour and look as if they were candescent.

I have seen the wind raise the sand on the furthest horizon, and the oasis gasp and shudder like a ship quaking in the storm. And in the streets of the little village, the men, lean and naked, were writhing in the throes of thirst and fever.

I have seen the bleaching carcasses of camels lying beside desolate tracks – abandoned camels which had been too weary to drag themselves along and which had already begun to rot, covered with flies and giving out an abominable stench.

I have seen evenings whose only song was the shrill creaking of insects.

119

And still I must speak of the desert:

Desert of alfa, haunt of grass-snakes, green plain, undulating in the wind.

Desert of stone; aridity; mica sparkles; beetles flit; reeds wither; everything crackles in the sun.

Desert of clay; here life might abound if only there were a little water. At the first rain everything turns green; and though the parched earth seems to have lost the habit of smiling, the grass is tenderer here and more fragrant than elsewhere. It is more eager to flower, to give out its fragrance more quickly, for fear the sun should wither it before it has time to seed; its loves are precipitate. The sun returns; the earth splits, crumbles, loses its water in every direction. Land ravaged by crevasses; during the rains all the water flows away into the ravines; too weak to retain it, humiliated land; desperately thirsty land.

Desert of sand – sand that moves like the waves of the sea; constantly shifting sand-dunes; hillocks like pyramids serve to guide the caravans from point to point; from the top of one, the top of another can be seen on the far horizon.

When the wind blows, the caravan stops; the camel-drivers take shelter beside their camels.

Desert of sand whence life is excluded; nothing exists in it but the palpitation of the wind, of the heat. The sand in the shade has the soft texture of velvet; in the evening it looks candescent and in the morning like ashes. There are valleys between the sand-hills which are dead-white; we rode through some of them on horseback; the sand closed over our tracks; at every fresh hill, we were so tired we thought we should never be able to get past it.

I have passionately loved you, desert of sand. Ah! let your tiniest particle of dust, there where it lies, speak to us of the whole universe! What life do you remember, dust? Of what love are you the remnant? The dust demands that we praise it.

My soul, what did you see on the sand?
Bleached bones – empty shells . . .

One morning we reached a sand-hill high enough to shelter us from the sun. We sat down. The shade was almost cool and reeds grew there charmingly.

But what shall I say of the night? What of the night?

The night is a slow sea-voyage.
The waves are less blue than the sand.
The sand was more luminous than the sky.
There are certain nights when, one by one, each particular star seemed to me the most beautiful.
Saul, in the desert, looking for his asses. – You did not find your asses, but instead of them, the kingdom you were not looking for.

The satisfaction of feeding vermin on one's person.
Life for us had a

WILD AND SUDDEN FLAVOUR

and I am glad that happiness here
should be like an efflorescence
upon things dead.

BOOK VIII

Our acts are attached to us as its glimmer is to phosphorus. They consume us, it is true, but they make our splendour.

My mind, you have been transported to prodigious heights during your fabulous excursions.

O my heart, I have ministered abundantly to your thirst!

My body, I have surfeited you with love.

In vain, now that I am at rest, I try to count my riches. I have none.

I sometimes look into the past for some set of memories out of which to make myself a story, but there are none in which I can recognize myself, none that can contain my overflowing life. I realize then that I only live in each fresh succeeding moment. What people call 'withdrawing into oneself' is to me an impossible constraint; I can no longer understand the word '*solitude*'; to be alone with myself is to be nobody; I am peopled. For that matter, I am never at home save everywhere, and desire always drives me out. The most beautiful memory seems to me nothing but a piece of wreckage left by happiness. The least drop of water – even a tear – if it wets my hand, is a more precious reality.

*   *
*

I think of you, Menalcas!

Tell me! For what seas is your foam-bespattered ship making now?

Won't you soon return, Menalcas, laden with insolent wealth and eager to re-awaken the thirst of my desires? If I am now at rest, it is not thanks to your riches . . . No; you taught me never to rest. Aren't you tired yet of that horribly wandering existence? As for me, I may have cried out in pain sometimes, but I am tired of nothing; and when my body is weary, it is my weakness that I blame; my desires had hoped I should be more enduring. Oh no! if I regret anything today,

125

it is to have left untasted so many fruits, left them to spoil and be lost to me – fruits which you, O God of love, our nourisher, had offered me. For the Gospels tell us, so I was taught, that what one casts away today will be returned to us a hundredfold hereafter ... Ah! of what use to me are more riches than my desire can grasp? For already I have known such violent delights that even the tiniest trifle more and I should have been incapable of tasting them.

*　*
*

> *It was reported that I was doing penance ... but what have I to do with repentance?*
>
> SAADI.

Yes, it is true – my youth was spent in darkness.
It is of *that* I repent;
The salt of the earth was not to my taste;
Nor that of the great salt seas.
I thought that *I* was the salt of the earth.
And I was afraid of losing my savour.
The salt of the sea does not lose its savour; but my lips have already grown too old to taste it. Ah! why did I not breathe the sea air when my soul was greedy for it? What wine will now suffice to make me drunk?

Nathaniel, ah! satisfy your joy while it gladdens your soul – and your desire of love while your lips are still sweet to kiss, and while your embrace is joyous.

For afterwards you will think, you will say, 'The fruit was there; its weight bowed down the tired branches; my mouth was there and watered for it; but my mouth would not open and my hands could not grasp it because they were clasped in prayer; and so my soul and body suffer now from a hopeless thirst. The time has gone hopelessly by.'

(Can it be true, Shulamite? Can it be true?
You were awaiting me and I did not know it!

You sought me and I did not hear you coming.)

Ah, youth! Man possesses you only once and the rest of his life recalls you.

(Pleasure knocked at my door. Desire answered in my heart; I knelt on without opening.)

The stream that flows past me may doubtless water many other fields and quench the thirst of many other lips. But what can I know of that? What can it bring me but a cooling that is transient and that leaves a burning behind it? Appearances of my pleasure, you will flow away like water. And if the flow of water is to be here renewed, let it bring a draught where coolness may be abiding.

Inexhaustible freshness of rivers, unceasing gush of streams, how unlike you are to that little basinful of captured water in which I once dipped my hands, and which afterwards had to be thrown away because it was no longer cool! Captured water, you are like the wisdom of man. Wisdom of man, you have not the inexhaustible freshness of rivers.

Sleeplessness.

Longings. Longings; fever; past and gone hours of youth ... A burning thirst for all you call Sin.

There was a dog disconsolately baying the moon.

There was a cat wailing like an infant.

The town was at last going to taste a little calm before waking next morning with all its hopes revived.

I remember those bygone hours; my bare feet on the tiles; I leant my head on the wet iron railings of the balcony; my flesh in the moonlight shone like a marvellous fruit ripe for picking. Longings! you were our blight. ... Over-ripe fruit! we did not put our teeth into you until our thirst had grown agonizing and its fierceness intolerable. Rotten fruit! you filled our mouths with a poisonous sickliness; you profoundly disturbed my soul. Happy the man who tastes you while he is young, while your flesh is still firm, and who sucks your love-perfumed milk without delaying, so that he may run on his way refreshed – that way which for us will be a toilsome journey to the end.

(True it is that I have done my best to arrest the cruel wasting of my soul; but it was only by the wasting of my senses that I was able to distract it from its God; it was busied with him night and day; it ingeniously invented difficult prayers; it wore itself out with fervour.)

From what tomb have I escaped this morning? (The seabirds are bathing and stretching their wings.) And the image of life for me, ah, Nathaniel! is a fruit rich in flavour on lips thirsty with longing.

*   *
*

There were nights when it was impossible to sleep.

There were long watches – waiting – how often one did not know for what? I lay on my bed trying in vain to sleep, my limbs aching with fatigue and as if they had been dislocated by love. And sometimes I sought, beyond the pleasure of the flesh, as it were another, further, more secret pleasure.

. . . My thirst increased from hour to hour in proportion as I drank. At last it became so vehement that I could have wept with desire.

. . . My senses were worn to transparency, and when in the morning I went down to the town, the azure of the sky penetrated me.

My teeth, horribly set on edge by biting my lips, their tips as it were worn away. And my temples fallen in as though by internal suction. The smell of a field of flowering onions was within an ace of making me vomit.

Sleeplessness.

And in the night a voice was heard weeping and wailing. 'Ah!' it wept, 'this is the fruit of those pestiferous flowers: it is sweet.' Henceforth it is on the roads I shall walk with the vague tedium of my desire. Your comfortable rooms stifle me, and I am sick of your beds. Henceforth stop seeking an object for your interminable wanderings. . . .

My thirst had becomes so intense that I drank a whole glassful of that nauseous water before I noticed, alas! how nauseous it was . . . O Shulamite! for me you have been like the fruit that has ripened in the shade of a little walled garden.

Ah! thought I, all humanity tosses wearily between thirst for sleep and thirst for pleasure. After the fearful tension, the fierce concentration, and then the flagging of the flesh, one's only thought is to sleep. Ah, sleep! Ah! if only we were not wakened into life again by a fresh onslaught of desire.

And all humanity tosses like a sick man who seeks relief from suffering by turning in his bed.

. . . Then, after a few weeks of labour, eternities of rest.

. . . As if one could keep on one's clothing in death! (Simplification.) And we shall die — as though we were undressing to go to sleep.

Menalcas, Menalcas, I think of you!

Yes, I know that I said, 'What does it matter? Here — or — there — we shall be equally happy.'

. . . Now, out there, the evening would be closing in . . .

. . . Oh, if the stream of time could run backwards to its source and the past return! Nathaniel, how I wish I could take you back with me to those love-filled hours of my youth when life flowed in me like honey. Will the soul ever find consolation for having tasted such happiness? For it was I who was there, in those gardens — I, my very self; it was I who heard the piping of that reed, who breathed the scent of those flowers, it was I who saw, who touched that boy — and indeed every recurrent spring brings with it a recurrence of those pleasures — but the man I was — that other man, ah! how can I become him again? (Now the rain is falling on the roofs of the city; my room is solitary.) It is the hour when Lossif's flocks would be coming home; they came down from the hills; the desert in the west was full of the golden sunset; the evening was still . . . now; (now).

Athman, I think of you; Biskra, I think of your palm-trees –
Touggourt, of your sands. Oases! does the parching wind of
the desert still play in your rustling palms? Heat-cleft pomegranates! do you still drop your harsh seeds on to the ground?

Chetma, I remember your cool streams and the hot spring
which it made one perspire only to be near. El Kantara, golden
bridge, I remember your resonant mornings and your ecstatic
evenings. Zaghouan, I can see your fig-trees and your oleanders; Kairouan, your nopals; Sousse, your olive-trees. I
dream of your desolation Oumach, ruined town, swamp-
girdled walls – and of yours, Droh, haunt of eagles, fierce
village, hoarse-voiced gully.

Lofty Chegga, do you still gaze at the desert? M'rayer, do
you dip your frail wizened tamarisks in the chott? Megarine,
do you drink deep of your brackish waters? Temassine, are
you still wilting in the sun?

I remember near Enfida a barren rock from which honey
poured down in the spring-time; close by was a well where
beautiful women, almost naked, came to draw water.

Are you still there, Athman's little house, now, in the moonlight? Still half-ruined? House where your mother sat weav-
ing, where your sister, Amhour's wife, used to sing or tell
stories; where the brood of turtle-doves cooed, softly, joy-
ously, all night long beside the grey and sluggish water?

O longing! How many sleepless nights I have spent, because I was rapt in a dream which took the place of sleep!
Oh! if there are evening mists, sweet pipings under the palm-
trees, white garments in the darkness of the paths, soft shade
near the blazing light – it is there I will go . . .

Little lamp of earth and oil! the night wind teases your
flame; vanished window; simple embrasure of sky; calm night
above the roofs; moon.

At times, in the emptied streets below, is heard the clatter of
an omnibus, a carriage; and in the distance the sound of trains
leaving the city, trains whistling, trains fleeing – and the
great city waiting for the day . . .

Shadow of the balcony on the floor, vacillation of the flame on the white page. Quiet breathing.

The moon is hidden now; the garden below me is a pool of green ... A sob; close-pressed lips; overwhelming convictions; anguish of thought. What am I to say? *Things that are true.* OTHER PEOPLE – the importance of *their* lives. Let me speak to *them*.

HYMN

To M. A. G.

SHE turned her eyes towards the rising stars.

'I know all their names,' said she; 'each of them has many; they have different virtues. Their progress, which to us seems calm, is swift and makes their burning. Their restless ardour is the cause of the violence of their speed, and their splendour its effect. An inner will drives and directs them; a lovely zeal burns and consumes them; it is that that gives them their radiance and their beauty.

'They are all bound, each to each, by ties which are virtues and powers, so that each depends on the other and the other on all. The path of each is traced and each of them finds its own path. None can leave it without turning aside all the others, for each has the care of each. And each one chooses the path it is bound to follow; its duty must be willing, and that path which seems to us ordained is the path that each prefers, for they are of one perfect mind. A dazzling love guides them; their choice determines the laws; on them we depend; from them there is no escape.'

ENVOI

AND now, Nathaniel, throw away my book. Shake yourself
free of it. Leave me. Leave me; now you are in my way; you
hamper me; I have exaggerated my love for you and it occu-
pies me too much. I am tired of pretending I can educate anyone. When have I said that I wanted you to be like me? It is
because you differ from me that I love you; the only thing I
love in you is what differs from me. Educate! Whom should I
educate but myself? Yes, Nathaniel, I have educated my self
interminably. And I have not done yet. I only esteem myself
for my possibilities.

Nathaniel, throw away my book; do not let it satisfy you.
Do not think *your* truth can be found by anyone else; be
ashamed of nothing more than of that. If I found your food
for you, you would have no appetite for it; if I made your bed,
you would not be able to sleep in it.

Throw away my book; say to yourself that it is only *one* of
the thousand possible postures in life. Look for your own. Do
not do what someone else could do as well as you. Do not say,
do not write what someone else could say, could write as well
as you. Care for nothing in yourself but what you feel exists
nowhere else, and out of yourself create, impatiently or
patiently, ah! the most irreplaceable of beings.

LATER FRUITS OF THE EARTH
Les Nouvelles Nourritures
(1935)

BOOK I

I

You who will come when I shall have ceased to hear the noises of this earth and to taste its dew upon my lips — you who will perhaps some day read me — it is for you I write these pages; for perhaps you are not sufficiently amazed at being alive; you do not wonder as you should at this astounding miracle of your life. I sometimes feel that it is with my thirst that you will drink, and that what inclines you to that other creature you caress is my own desire.

(I marvel how desire, when it is a lover's, loses precision. My love enveloped so diffusedly and so simultaneously the whole of the beloved's body, that had I been Jupiter, I should have changed into a cloud without even being aware of it.)

The wandering breeze has stirred
The flowers. My heart has heard
The song of the first morning of the world.

Early elation,
Youthful sunshine,
Petals of blossom clammy
With dewy wine ...

Delay not to follow
The tenderest invitation,
Welcome the coming day's
Gentle invasion.

The sweet insidious airs
So mildly move,
Must not the shyest heart
Now yield to love?

That man is born for happiness,
Is what all nature teaches.

An all-pervading joy suffuses the earth and the earth exudes it at the sun's call. It is joy that thrills the atmosphere in which the elements come to life and, still submissive, make their escape from the primal rigour. . . . Lovely complexities are born from the interweaving of the laws of nature — the seasons, the movement of the tides, the vapours that are drawn up and showered down again in streams, the tranquil alternation of the days, the periodic recurrence of the winds — everything as it comes into being, sways to and fro in a harmonious rhythm. Everything is prepared for the organization of joy, and soon joy is born; it flutters unwittingly in the leaf, it takes name and diversity, becomes fragrance in the flower, flavour in the fruit, a conscious voice in the bird. So that the return, the informing and then the disappearance of life imitate the circuitous passage of water which evaporates in the sunshine and then regathers again to fall in the shower.

Each animal is nothing but a parcel of joy.

Everything is glad to be and every being rejoices. You call it fruit when joy becomes succulence, bird when it is turned into song.

All nature indeed teaches that man is born for happiness. It is the effort after pleasure that makes the plant germinate, fills the hive with honey, and the human heart with love.

Wood-pigeons that exult among the trees,
Branches that sway gently in the breeze,
White sails that lean upon the breeze-tossed sea,
The sea that shines between the swaying trees,
The crested waves that whiten in the breeze —
And all this laughter, azure, light,
Are my heart's tale, telling to thine, my sister,
Its delight.

I have no idea who could have put me on to this earth. I have been told it was God; and if it was not God, who could it have been?

It is true that I feel so intense a joy in existing that sometimes I think I must have already wanted to be alive even before I was.

But we will put off theological discussions till winter, for they are really enough to put one in a bad temper.

A clean sheet. I have swept everything away. Over and done with! I stand naked upon virgin soil beneath an emptied Heaven, ready for fresh occupants.

Pooh! I know you, Phoibos! You spread your luxuriant locks over the silver-frosted grass. Come with your liberator's bow. Your golden dart penetrates my closed eyelids, strikes at the shades, triumphs; and the monster lurking within is vanquished. Bring colour and ardour to my flesh, thirst to my lips, dazzlement to my heart. Of all the silken ladders you fling from the zenith to the earth, I will seize the loveliest. I have lost footing on the ground. I swing from the extremity of a sun-beam.

O boy whom I love; I will carry you with me in my flight. Seize the sunbeam with an agile hand; behold the day-star! Away with your ballast! Let not the weight of the lightest past be a drag upon your freedom.

No more delay! No more delay! O obstructed road! I push on. It is my turn. The sunbeam has signed to me; my desire is the surest of guides and this morning I am in love with the whole world.

A thousand luminous threads cross and intertwine on my heart. Out of thousands of fragile perceptions I weave a miraculous garment. Through it the god laughs and I smile back to the god. Who was it said that great Pan was dead? I saw him through the mist of my breath. My lips are stretched towards him. Was it not he who whispered in my ear this morning, 'What are you waiting for?'

With mind and hand I brush aside all intercepting veils, so that there shall be nothing before me but what is brilliant and bare.

Spring, full of indolent days,
Be merciful, I pray.
My yielding heart obeys
Your languorous sway,
And with the wavering wind
Floats my irresolute mind.

Of honied sweets a stream
Pours down on me.
Only through veils of dream
Oh to hear! Oh to see!

Through my soft-lidded sight
I feel and greet thy light.

Warm sun's caress,
Pardon my idleness.

Take me, indulgent sun,
Defenceless and undone.

A new Adam, it is I today who baptize. This river is my thirst; this shady grove my sleep; this naked boy my desire. In this bird's song, my love finds its voice. My heart murmurs in this hive. Displaceable horizon, be my limit; beneath the slanting rays, you recede, you grow vague, you grow blue.

Of love and thought here is the subtle confluence.

The white page gleams before me.

And as God becomes man, so my idea clothes itself, submissive to the laws of rhythm.

A painter who creates anew, I here spread the image of my perfect happiness in the most tremulous, the most vivid of my colours.

I will catch at words by their wings only. Is it you, my woodpigeon, my joy? Ah! do not yet, do not yet fly back to heaven. Alight here. Here rest.

I am lying on the ground. Near me a branch with its load of bursting fruit is bowed down to the ground; it touches the grass; it lightly caresses the tenderest blade of grass. The weight of a pigeon's cooing sways it.

I WRITE so that a youth coming after me and like what I was at sixteen, only freer, more accomplished, may find here an answer to his enquiring heart. But what will his question be?

I have not come much into contact with my generation, and my contemporaries' games have never much amused me. I look beyond the present. I push forward. I foresee a time when everything that seems vital to us today will be barely comprehensible.

I dream of new harmonies – a subtler, franker art of words, not rhetorical, not seeking to prove anything.

Oh! who will deliver my mind from the heavy chains of logic? My sincerest emotion is distorted as soon as I express it.

LIFE might be more beautiful than men consent to make it. Wisdom lies not in reason but in love. Ah! I have hitherto lived over-prudently. One must be lawless to hear aright the new law. O deliverance! O liberty! As far as my desire is able to reach, so far will I go. O you whom I love, come with me; thus far I will carry you – so that you may go farther still.

WE amused ourselves all day long by executing the various actions of our lives like a dance, in the manner of a perfect gymnast, whose ideal would be to do nothing that was not harmonious and rhythmical. Mark would fetch water from the pump, pump it and carry up the bucket according to a carefully thought out rhythm. We studied all the movements necessary for fetching a bottle from the cellar, uncorking and drinking it; we decomposed them. We clinked our glasses in cadence. We invented steps too to extricate ourselves from the difficult situations of life; some to denote private troubles; some to dissemble them. There was the *pas de basque* of condolences and another of congratulations. There was the *rigodon* of wild hopes and the minuet called 'legitimate aspirations'. As in famous ballets, there was the bickering step, the quarrel step, the reconciliation step. We were particularly good at *ensembles*; but the step of the perfect pal was a *pas seul*. The most amusing step we invented was the one of running down to bathe; we did it together across the whole length of the big field; the movement was in double quick time because we wanted to be in a sweat when we arrived; it was done in huge leaps which were made easy by the slope of the ground, with one hand stretched in front of us like people running to catch a tram, and the other holding up our loose bath-robes. We reached the water panting and plunged in at once, shouting with laughter and reciting Mallarmé.

But all this you will say, in spite of its lyrical spirit, was a little lacking in *laisser-aller*. . . . Ah! I was forgetting our sudden *entrechat* of spontaneity.

From the day that I succeeded in persuading myself that I had no need to be happy, happiness began to dwell in me; yes, from the day I persuaded myself that I needed nothing in order to be happy. After I had struck my pick at the roots of selfishness, I felt that a fountain of joy had sprung up from my heart so abundant that I should be able to quench everybody else's thirst with it. I understood that the best teaching was example. I took up my happiness as a vocation.

What! I thought then, if my soul must dissolve at the same time as my body, let me realize my joy as quickly as possible. If by chance my soul is immortal, shall I not have eternity to spend on what can be of no interest to my senses? Am I to disdain this beautiful country through which I am passing, to reject its delights, because they will soon be taken from me? The swifter my passage the more eager let my eyes be; the more precipitate my flight, the more immediate be my embrace. Why, lover of a moment, should I clasp less fondly what I know I cannot keep? Inconstant soul, hasten! Remember that the loveliest flower is the one that soonest fades. Breathe its perfume quickly. The everlasting has no scent.

Soul born for joy, fear nothing but what may dim the brightness of your song.

But now I understand that God, permanently present in all that passes, dwells not in the object but in love; and now I know how to enjoy the quiet of eternity in the fleeting moment.

If you feel that you cannot remain in this state of joy, do not make too great an effort to attain it.

> *Greet me as I awake,*
> *Dazzling and lovely light!*
> *I claim no immaterial*
> *Delight.*
>
> *As Ariel winged and free,*
> *I love you, cloudless sky,*
> *But even in Heaven's blue,*
> *If caught, I die.*
>
> *Can anything be more*
> *Substantial than this?*
> *To listen is to hear —*
> *To hear and not to miss.*
>
> *Haste then, oh! let me haste*
> *Those honied sweets to taste.*

This morning I am like the man who knows that his pen is a little too full of ink and, for fear of making a blot, traces a garland of words.

II

It is my grateful heart that makes me invent God anew every day. No sooner am I awake than astonishment fills me that I exist, and my wonder is unceasing. Why does the cessation of pain bring less joy than the end of joy causes regret? It is because in every grief we remember the happiness it deprives us of, while in the bosom of happiness it never occurs to us to think of the sorrows we are spared; it is because it is natural to us to be happy.

A certain sum of happiness is due to each creature according to the capacity of his heart and senses to support it. However little I am deprived of this, I am cheated. I do not know whether I asked for life before I existed, but now that I am alive, I claim all my due. But gratitude is so sweet to me and so sweet my necessity of loving that the air's slightest caress awakes a paean of thanks in my heart. The need of gratitude teaches me to make happiness out of everything that comes to me.

The fear of stumbling makes our minds cling to the railing of logic. There is logic and there is what escapes logic. (Want of logic irritates me, but excess of logic exhausts me.) Some people reason rightly, and some let others be right without reasoning. (If my reason tells my heart that it is wrong to beat, I tell it that it is right against reason.) There are some people who can do without living and others who can do without being in the right. The point where logic fails is the point where I begin to be conscious of myself. O dearest, loveliest of my thoughts! why should I try any more to legalize your birth? Did I not read in Plutarch this morning at the beginning of the lives of Romulus and Theseus, that those two great founders of cities passed as the sons of Gods because their birth was secret and clandestine? . . .

I am in bondage to my past. Not a gesture today but was determined by what I was yesterday. But who I am at this moment, I, instantaneous, fleeting, irreplaceable, I escape . . .

Oh! to be able to escape from myself! I would overleap the barriers behind which self-respect has confined me. My nostril dilates to the wind. Oh! to weigh anchor, bound for the wildest adventure . . . And that it should be without consequence for the future.

My mind boggles at the word — consequence. Consequence of our acts. Consequence with ourselves. Am I to expect nothing from myself but a sequel? Consequence — compromise — a road traced beforehand. I want now not to walk but to leap. With the spring of my muscles to push off, to reject my past; to have no more promises to keep; I have made too many! Future, how I should love you, if you could be unfaithful!

What wind from sea or mountain will carry you, my soaring thoughts? Blue bird, fluttering and beating your wings on the sheer extremity of that rock, you advance as far as the present can carry you, and already, your straining eyes take flight, you escape into the future.

O new anxieties! Questions that have never yet been put! . . . I am weary with yesterday's struggle; I have more than exhausted its bitterness; I have ceased to believe in it; I lean over the future's gulf without giddiness. Winds of the abyss, bear me away!

III

Every affirmation is accomplished in abnegation. Everything you resign within you will come to life. All affirmation of self is self-destroying; all self-denial is self-affirming. Perfect possession is only to be proved by the perfect gift. It is you who are possessed by all you will not give. Without sacrifice there is no resurrection. Nothing grows and blooms save by giving. All you try to save in yourself wastes and perishes.

How do you know the fruit is ripe? Because it leaves the bough. All things ripen for the giving's sake and in the giving are consummated.

O luscious fruit wrapped round with delight, I know that in order to germinate you must sacrifice yourself. Let it die then, let it die, that delicious envelope! Let it die, that sweet and juicy flesh, for it belongs to the earth. Let it die that you may live. I know that 'except it die it abideth alone'.

Oh Lord! grant me not to wait for death in order to die.

It is renunciation that brings all virtue to perfection. The extreme succulence of the fruit is its effort towards germination.

True eloquence renounces eloquence; the individual is never so self-expressive as in self-forgetfulness. The thought of self is a hindrance to self. I never admire beauty so much as when it is unconscious of being beautiful. That line is most touching that is least assertive. Christ in truth becomes God by renouncing his divinity. And conversely, God, by renouncing himself in Christ, becomes God.

ENCOUNTERS

TO JEAN-PAUL ALLÉGRET

I

THAT day as we were walking about Paris at haphazard, just as the fancy led us, we met – do you remember? – in the Rue de Seine, a poor Negro, whom we couldn't help stopping to look at. It was just outside Fischbacher's bookshop. (I mention this because by dint of being poetical one sometimes ends by being vague.) And to give ourselves an excuse for stopping, we pretended to be looking at the shop-window; but it was really the Negro we were looking at. He was poor – no doubt about that! And he looked all the poorer because of his efforts not to seem so; for he was a Negro who was very much concerned about his dignity. He had on a top hat and a real frock-coat; but the hat was like a circus performer's and the frock-coat was terribly threadbare; he wore linen, no doubt, but perhaps it only looked white because he was black; it was the lamentable state of his shoes in particular that showed his extreme poverty. He took tiny little steps as he walked, like someone who has nowhere to go, and who will soon not be able to go anywhere; and at every other step, he stopped, lifted his chimney-pot and fanned himself with it, though it was a cold day; then he took a grimy handkerchief out of his pocket and wiped his forehead with it, then he put it back again; he had a high bare forehead below a shock of silvery hair; his eyes were vague, like those of people who expect nothing more from life, and he seemed not to see the passers-by; but when one of them stopped to look at him, he quickly put on his hat for dignity's sake and started walking again. He had certainly just been to see a person from whom he had expected something that had just been refused him. He had the look people have who have lost all hope. He had the look of someone who is dying of hunger but who would rather die than again stoop to ask.

Certainly he wanted to prove – and to prove to himself – that being a Negro is not enough to make one consent to humiliation. Oh! I should have liked to follow him and find out where he was going. But he wasn't going anywhere. Oh! I should have liked to speak to him, but I didn't know how to without offending him. And then I didn't know how much you who were with me were interested in life and everything that is alive.

. . . Oh! all the same I ought to have spoken to him.

2

And it was that same day a little later that, as we were going home by the metro, we saw that likeable-looking little man who was carting round a bowl of fish. The bowl was covered with a piece of stuff which was open on one side to allow a sight of its contents, and the whole contraption was wrapped up in paper. It was impossible at first to make out what it was, but he was so careful with it that I asked him as a joke whether it was a bomb.

'Fish!' he said mysteriously, drawing me to the light. And as he was of an affable disposition and saw that we should like nothing better than to talk, 'I cover them up,' he went on, 'so as not to attract attention; but if you like pretty things – and you're an artist, surely – I'll show you.'

And carefully uncovering the bowl with the gesture of a mother changing her baby's napkins, 'It's my job,' he continued: 'I breed fish. See there! those little fellows are worth ten francs apiece. Tiny things! but you've no idea how rare they are. And so pretty too! Just look, when they catch a ray of light. There! Green! Blue! Pink! They've no colours of their own – they take them all in turn.'

There was nothing in the bowl of water but a dozen or so darting needles which one after the other flashed into irridescence as they passed by the opening in the stuff.

'And do you breed them?'

'Yes. And I breed a great many others too. But I don't take the others out with me. They're too delicate. Just think! I have some which cost fifty and sixty francs each. People come to see them in my own place. The fish never leave it till they're sold. Last week a rich collector bought one which cost a hundred and twenty francs. It was a China ciprin; it had three tails like a pasha! Are they difficult to breed? Of course. It's difficult to feed them and they're always getting liver complaints. Once a week they have to be put into Vichy water. It comes very expensive. Otherwise no; they breed like rabbits. Are you a collector, Monsieur? You ought to come and see me.'

And now I've lost his address. Oh, how sorry I am I didn't go!

3

'We must start from this point,' said he, 'that the most important inventions still remain to be discovered. They will come by the simple shedding of a fresh light – the simplest recognition of plain facts; for all the secrets of nature lie open to us and strike our eyes every day without our noticing them. The peoples of the future will pity us when they have learnt how to make use of the sun's light and heat – pity us for so laboriously extracting our light and fuel from the bowels of the earth and for wasting our coal without regard to coming generations. When will man learn to capture and canalize with industry and economy all the ill-distributed or superfluous heat from every torrid portion of the globe? The time will come. It'll come!' he went on pompously. 'It'll come when the earth begins to grow cold, for at that same moment coal will begin to get scarce.'

'But,' said I, to distract him from the gloomy meditations into which I saw he was again plunging, 'you speak too sagaciously not to be an inventor yourself.'

'Sir,' he went on at once, 'the greatest are not the best known. What, pray, is a Pasteur, a Lavoisier, a Pushkin compared to the inventor of the wheel, the needle, the top, and the man who first noticed that a child's hoop keeps upright as it rolls? To learn to use our eyes – that is what is wanted. But we live without looking. For instance, what an admirable invention is the pocket! But have you ever given it a thought? And yet everybody makes use of it. Observation, I tell you, is all that is needed. ... One moment,' he said suddenly, changing his tone and pulling me aside by my sleeve. 'You see that person who has just come into the room? Beware of him. The old buck has never made any discoveries himself, but he would like to rob other people of theirs.' (This was my friend C——, the head doctor of the asylum.) Look at him questioning that poor ecclesiastic – yes, that gentleman over there. He's dressed in ordinary clothes, but in reality he's a priest. *He's* a great inventor too. It's unfortunate we've fallen out. I think if we could have worked together, we might have done great things. But when I speak to him, he answers in what might just as well be Chinese. Besides, he's been avoiding me for some time past. Go up and speak to him presently when the old beau leaves him. You'll see. He knows a great many curious things, and if he had a little more *esprit de suite* in his ideas ... There! He's alone now. Go and speak to him.'

'Not before you tell me what you've invented.'

'You really want to know?'

He leant towards me, then, suddenly flinging back his head and shoulders, he said in a low voice and in a tone of the strangest gravity:

'I am the inventor of the button!'

As my friend C—— had now withdrawn, I went up to the bench where the 'gentleman' remained seated, his elbows on his knees and his head between his hands.

'Haven't I met you somewhere?' I asked by way of introduction.

'Yes, I think so,' he said, after taking a look at me. 'But tell me, wasn't it you who were talking just now to that poor ambassador? Yes, the person who's walking up and down by himself and is just going to turn his back. ... How is he? We were very good friends once upon a time – but he has a jealous disposition. Ever since he realized he couldn't do without me, he has taken a dislike to me.'

'How do you explain that?' I ventured to ask.

'Oh, my dear sir, it's easy to understand. He invented the

button. He no doubt told you so. But *I* am the inventor of the buttonhole.'

'So you have quarrelled?'

'Inevitably.'

IV

I do not find in the letter of the Gospels any actual prohibitions. But the important thing is that we should contemplate God with the clearest possible eyes, and I feel that every object on this earth that I covet becomes opaque by very reason of my coveting it, and that the whole world then loses its transparence, or else my eyes lose their clearness, so that God ceases to be perceptible to my soul, and by abandoning the Creator for the creature, my soul ceases to live in eternity and loses possession of the kingdom of God.

Lord Christ, I return to you as to God whose living form you are. I am weary of lying to my heart. It is you I find at every turn when I thought I was fleeing you, divine friend of my childhood. I am beginning to believe that none but you can satisfy my exacting heart. It is only the demon within me who denies that your teaching is perfect and that I can renounce all things save only you — for in renouncing all things, it is you I find.

Of very youth the Gate,
Threshold of Paradise,
My soul with joy elate,
Drunken with glad surprise,
In rapture of amaze,
For greater rapture prays.

Smooth the dividing space
That parts me, Lord, from Thee!
Exiled and in disgrace,
My soul remembers Thee . . .
Heighten my extasy!

The sandy desert keeps
Of a bare foot the trace,
My artless poem seeks
To snatch from rhyme a grace.

My soul in joyous ease
Swinging sublime
Floats upon rhythmic seas
Careless of time.

When laughing shrubs are drest
In their first wealth of flowers
The singing birds will nest
In the old oak's weeping bowers.

The leaves are stirred and shake
With laugh and song divine —
The drink with which I slake
My thirst is more than wine.

Flash, O too dazzling light,
Through my closed eyelids, Lord,
The brightness of thy Truth
Has pierced me like a sword.

ENCOUNTERS

It was in Florence on a festa day. What festa? I cannot call to mind. From my window, which looked on to one of the quays of the Arno between the Ponte San Trinità and the Ponte Vecchio, I was watching the crowd below, and waiting for the moment towards evening when it becomes more intensely alive, and when I should be seized with the desire to go down and mix with it. And as I was looking up stream, there came a rumour – people began running, and just at the very place on the Ponte Vecchio where the fringe of houses that edge it stops and leaves an empty gap right in the middle of the bridge, I saw the crowd hurrying, bending over the parapet, stretching out their arms and pointing to a small object which was floating away in the muddy waters of the river, disappearing in an eddy, reappearing again, to be finally carried away by the current. I went down. The passers-by I questioned said that a little girl had fallen into the water; her skirt had buoyed her up for a little, but by now she had disappeared. Boats had put out from the shore; men armed with boat-hooks searched the river till nightfall – in vain.

What! in this dense crowd, had there been no-one to notice the child, to hold her back? . . . I made my way to the Ponte Vecchio. At the very spot from which the little girl had just flung herself was a boy about fifteen years old who was answering the questions of the passers-by. He said he had seen the little girl suddenly climb over the balustrade; he had rushed forward and caught her by the arm and for some time had managed to hold her up over the river; the crowds behind him passed on without noticing anything; he had wanted to call for help, as he hadn't the strength to pull the child back on to the bridge by himself. But, 'No!' she had said, 'let me go,' and in such a heart-rending voice that in the end he had loosed his hold. He sobbed as he told his story.

(He himself was one of those poor children who would perhaps be less unhappy without a family. He was dressed in rags.

And I imagined that at the moment he was holding the little girl by the arm and trying to wrest her from death, feeling and sharing her despair, a despairing love had seized him too as it had her, and had opened Heaven for them both. It was out of pity he had let go. 'Prego . . . lasciatemi.')

People asked him whether he knew her; but no; it was the first time he had seen her; no-one knew who she was, and all the enquiries made in the days following were fruitless. The body was found. It was that of a girl of fourteen; very thin, and dressed in very wretched clothes. What would I not have given to know more about her – whether her father had a mistress or her mother a lover, and what support had suddenly failed her without which she was unable to live.

'But why,' Nathaniel asked me, 'this story in a book you dedicate to joy?'

I wish I could have told this story more simply still. Truly, I do not want a happiness that springs from wretchedness. Riches that leave another poor I do not want. If my clothes are stripped from others, I will go naked. Ah! Lord Christ, your table is open to all, and what makes the beauty of your banquet is that all are invited to it.

There are on this earth such immensities of misery, distress, poverty and horror that the happy man cannot think of it without feeling ashamed of his happiness. And yet no-one can do anything for the happiness of others if he cannot be happy himself. I feel an imperious obligation to be happy. But all happiness seems to me hateful which is obtained only at the expense of others and by possessions of which others are deprived. One step further and we come up against the tragic social question. All the arguments of my reason will not hold me back on the incline that leads to communism.[1] But what seems to me mistaken is to demand that a man who has possessions shall distribute them. What moonshine to expect that he will willingly resign the possessions to which his whole soul is attached! As for myself, I feel an aversion to every possession that is exclusive; my happiness is made of giving, and I shall not be left with much in hand for death to rob me of. The most I shall be deprived of are those many natural riches which cannot be appropriated and which are common to all. Of those I have taken my fill. As for the rest, I prefer the ordinary of a roadside inn to the best served table, the public gardens to the finest park enclosed by walls, and the book I am not afraid to take out with me on a walk to the rarest edition. And if I had to be alone to look at a picture, the finer it was the more my pleasure would be outweighed by my sadness.

My happiness is to increase other people's. To be happy myself I need the happiness of all.

1. On this incline which seems to me to lead upwards, my reason has now joined my heart. Oh! more than that. It is my reason now that leads the way. And if sometimes I am sorry to see that some communists are only theorists, that other error which tends to make communism a matter of sentiment seems to me quite as grave (March, 1935).

I admired – I have not done admiring – a superhuman effort in the Gospels towards joy. The first reported word of Christ's is 'Beatus ...'. His first miracle is the changing of water into wine. (The true Christian is he whom pure water suffices to intoxicate. It is within a man's self that the miracle of Cana is repeated.) It required men's abominable interpretation to base on the Gospels the worship, the sanctification of grief and pain. Because Christ said, 'Come unto me all that travail and are heavy-laden, and I will refresh you,' people have believed that it was necessary to travail and be heavy-laden in order to come to him; and the refreshment he offered they turned into 'indulgences'.

It has long seemed to me that joy is rarer, more difficult, lovelier than sadness. And when I had made this discovery, which is doubtless the most important one that can be made in this life, joy became to me not only a natural need (which it was already) but also indeed a moral obligation. It seemed to me that the best, the surest way of spreading happiness about one was to give an image of it oneself and I resolved to be happy.

'He who is happy,' I once wrote, 'and who yet thinks, he shall be called the true worthy.' For what good to me is a happiness built upon ignorance? Christ's first word is to embrace sadness itself in joy: 'Blessed are those who weep.' *And he has little understanding of this word who sees in it nothing but an encouragement to weep!*

BOOK II

I THINK, therefore I am.

It is the 'therefore' *I shy at.*

I think *and I am; it would be truer to say:*

I feel, therefore I am – or even: I believe, therefore I am – for it comes to saying:

I think that I am.

I believe that I am.

I feel that I am.

Now of these three propositions, the last seems to me the truest – in fact, the only one that is true; for after all 'I think that I am' *does not perhaps absolutely imply that I am. Nor does* 'I believe that I am.' *It is as rash to jump from this to that as to make* 'I believe that God is' *a proof of God's existence. Whereas* 'I feel that I am' *is a case in which I am judge and party. How can I be mistaken here?*

I think therefore that I am – *I think that* I am, *therefore I am. For I must think something:*

Ex. I think that God exists

or

I think that the angles of a triangle are equal to two right angles, therefore I am.

Then it is the I *that is impossible to establish. I keep to the neuter then and say* 'therefore it *is.*'

I think, therefore I am.

I might just as well say: I suffer, or I breathe or I feel, therefore I am. *For if it is impossible to think without being, it is quite possible to be without thinking.*

But as long as I only feel, I am without thinking that I am. By this act of thinking I become conscious of being; but at the same moment I cease to be simply being, I am thinking.

I think, therefore I am *is equivalent to I think that I am, and the* 'therefore', *like the beam of the balance weighs nothing. In each of the two scales there is only what I have put into it – namely, the same thing.* $X = X$. *I change the terms about in vain – nothing comes of it –*

173

except after a time a bad headache and a great longing to go out for a walk.

Some of the 'problems' which agitate us are by no means insignificant, but simply insoluble — and to make our decision depend on their solution is madness. So let's pass on.

'But before any action, I must know why I am on this earth, whether God exists and whether he sees us, for if he does, I cannot do without his notice; I must know first of all whether . . .'

'Find out then! Find out! But in the mean time you won't be acting.'

Let us put all this cumbersome luggage in the cloak-room as quickly as possible — and then, like Edouard, make haste to lose the ticket.[1]

1. See *The Coiners* (Les Faux Monnayeurs) by André Gide. (*Translator's note.*)

It is much more difficult than one thinks not to believe in God. One must never really have looked at nature. The slightest agitation of matter . . . Why should it stir and towards what? But this impregnation takes me quite as far from your creed as it does from atheism. That matter should be penetrable and ductile and open to mind, that mind should be so intermingled with matter as to make one with it – you may call my amazement at this religious, if you like. I am amazed at everything on this earth. Let us call my stupefaction worship. Very well. But how much further does it take us? Not only do I not see your God in any of all this, but on the contrary I see everywhere manifested that he cannot *be in it – that he* is *not in it.*

I am ready to call everything Divine which God himself could not alter.

This formula which is inspired (its last words, at any rate) by a sentence of Goethe's,[1] *has the advantage, not so much of implying belief in God, as the impossibility of admitting a God in opposition to the laws of nature (to himself, in fact) – a God who would not be identical with them.*

'How does this differ from Spinoza?' you ask.

I have no desire it should differ from Spinoza. I have already quoted Goethe who gladly recognized his debt to Spinoza. Everybody owes something of himself to someone else. There are certain minds to whom I am related and attached and whom I take pleasure in revering as much as you revere the Fathers of your church. But whereas your tradition goes back to a divine revelation and for that very reason is forbidden all liberty of thought, this other tradition, being purely human, not only leaves my thought its independence, but encourages it and incites me to accept nothing as true that I have not first of all verified *myself unless it is not in my power to verify – and this by no means betokens pride; it may even co-exist with a very patient and prudent and even diffident humble-mindedness, but it loathes the false modesty that consists in thinking man incapable of attaining any truth by himself or without the miraculous intervention of divine revelation.*

1. *Dichtung und Wahrheit*, Book XVI.

ENCOUNTERS

'There has been a great deal of talk about me lately,' said God to me. 'Quite a number of reports have reached me up here. It has become rather tiresome, in fact. Yes, I know. I'm the fashion. But as often as not I don't at all like what people say of me – and sometimes I don't even understand it. Now you who are one of them – for you pique yourself on your literature, don't you? – you might just tell me who wrote the little sentence which among all the other nonsense quite pleased me: "People ought only to talk about God naturally."'

'The little sentence is mine,' I said, blushing.

'Very good. Then listen,' said God, who ever since has treated me like an old friend. 'Some people are always wanting me to interfere and disturb the existing order of things on their behalf. But it would confuse things too much and besides be cheating not to keep my own laws. Let such people learn to submit to them a little better. Let them understand that that is the way they may best profit by them. Man can do a great deal more than he imagines.'

'Man is in a mess,' said I.

'Let him get out of it,' God went on. 'It's to show him my esteem that I leave him to his own devices.'

'Between ourselves,' he said too, 'it didn't give me as much trouble as all that. It came quite naturally. Everything arose as it were in spite of myself out of the first few premisses. So that the smallest bud, as it developed, explains me to myself better than all the ratiocinations of the theologians. Diffused throughout my creation, I hide and lose and find myself again in it unceasingly, so inextricably intermingled with it that I doubt whether without it I should really exist; in it I test my own possibilities. But it is rather in the brain of man that the diffused whole takes on number; for sounds, colours, perfumes exist only in relation to man; and the loveliest dawn, the wind's most melodious song and the reflection of the sky on the waters and the rippling of the waves, are only empty talk as long as man has not registered them and his senses turned them into harmony. It is refracted from this sensitive mirror that my whole creation is set vibrating with colour and emotion. . . .'

'I must own,' he said too, 'that men have greatly disappointed me. On pretext of better worshipping me those who are fondest of calling themselves my children turn their back upon all the things I have prepared for them on this earth. Yes, the very ones who call me their father! How can they suppose I take pleasure in seeing them peak and pine and deny themselves for the love of me? . . . A fine figure of fun it makes of me!

'I have hidden away my most delightful secrets as you hide Easter eggs under the bushes in the garden for your children to find. Those who take a little trouble to look for them are the ones I like best.'

When I consider and weigh this word of God that I use, I am obliged to acknowledge that it is practically empty of substance — which is the very thing that makes it so convenient for me to use. A vessel of indefinite shape whose confining limits can be indefinitely extended, it contains whatever each of us chooses to put into it, but contains only whatever each of us puts in. If I pour in omnipotence, how shall I not feel awe for this receptacle? And love, if I fill it with care for myself and lovingkindness for each of us? If I lend it the thunderbolt and gird it with the blade of lightning, it is no longer the storm that makes me tremble with terror, but God.

Prudence, conscience, kindness, I cannot possibly imagine any of these things apart from man. That man, detaching all these things from himself, may imagine them very vaguely as things in themselves — that is, in the abstract — and fashion God with them, is possible; it is possible even for him to imagine that God is the beginning, that absolute being comes first, and that reality is caused by it and in turn becomes its cause — in short, that the Creator has need of the creature, for if he created nothing he would not be a creator. So that both the one and the other are in a state of such perfect relationship and interdependence that it may be said that the one could not exist without the other, the creator without the created, and that man could not have greater need of God than God of man, and that it is easier to imagine nothing at all than the one without the other.

I am God's; he is mine; we are. But in thinking this, I only make one with the whole of creation; I am dissolved and absorbed in prolix humanity.

'As for the *Bon Dieu*,' said the charming girl to me, 'have it your own way. There! I'll give him up to you; for I feel you're a person it's no use arguing with. And besides there's no getting away from God; he will always find out his own, as they say. And you belong to him whether you will or no. The curé told me so only yesterday. "God will save you in spite of yourself." For you're good, so how can you say you don't love the *Bon Dieu*? If only you weren't so obstinate, you'd soon understand that your own goodness is part of his and that everything that's good in you comes from him. . . . But it's the Blessed Virgin I've come to speak to you about today. No! upon my word, I can't let you off there! And I should very much like to know how you – poet as you are – can possibly manage not to love her. In reality you love her without realizing it – or rather without admitting it to yourself, because of your pride. No, really, it's too pigheaded of you! Why can't you simply acknowledge that the silvery mist that floats over the slumbering meadows in the early morning is just her dress? That the sudden calm that stills the troubled waves is nothing but her feet – those pure subduers of the serpent? And the ray of light you admire that falls trembling from the stars and makes the water of the pool sparkle in the dark, and is reflected in your heart, is her glance. And the melodious rustle of the leaves stirring so softly in the wind is her voice in your heart. She herself can only be seen by those whose sole desire is purity; and it is in order to behold her image in the hearts of men that she makes herself the guardian of their purity. I have never caught sight of her myself – no, not yet. But I know that it is she and the love I bear her that drive away all that threatens to soil me. . . . Come now, be a dear! Consent to acknowledge – to love her, for it's the same thing. It would give me so much pleasure! . . . And then the Blessed Virgin is so sweet that she doesn't mind my preferring her little child Jesus to her. Oh! as for him! . . . But while I love him, I never forget that he's her son. Indeed one can't love one without the other – and the Holy Ghost too. No really, the more I think of it, the less I understand your objections, and if I dared speak my mind – I can't help thinking you're rather foolish about it all.'

'Then let's talk of something else,' I said.

I acknowledge that for a long time I used the word God *as a kind of dumping ground for all my vaguest concepts. The result was something very different from Francis Jammes' God with a long white beard, but with hardly more existence. And as it happens that old people lose successively hair and teeth, sight, memory and finally life itself, my God as he grew old (but it was I who grew old not he) lost all the attributes with which I had formerly endowed him, and to begin – or end – with, his existence, or if you prefer it, his reality. If I stopped thinking of him, he stopped existing. It was solely my worship that created him. It* could do without him *– he could not do without it. The whole thing turned into a play of mirrors which ceased to amuse me when I understood it was carried on entirely at my expense. And for a little time longer this divine remnant attempted to take refuge – without any personal attributes – in beauty, the harmony of number, the* conatus vivendi *of nature. . . . At the present moment I see no particular interest in talking of it.*

But all the same, what in those days I called God – that confused mass of notions, sentiments, appeals, and answers to those appeals, which I now know existed only through and in me – all of this seems to me now, when I think of it, much more worthy of interest than the rest of the world and myself and the whole of humanity.

What an absurd conception of the world and of life it is that causes three quarters of our misery! Out of attachment to the past we refuse to understand that tomorrow's happiness is only possible if today's makes room for it, that every wave owes the beauty of its curve to the retreat of the one that precedes it, that every flower must fade in order to bear its fruit, and unless the fruit falls and dies, it cannot produce future flowerings, so that spring itself is founded upon winter's loss.

These considerations induce me — have always induced me — to listen more attentively to the teaching of natural history than to that of the history of mankind. I consider the latter far less profitable; there is always an element of chance in it.

The development of the humblest weed obeys immutable laws which escape human logic, or at any rate, are not confined to it. Experiments in this case may be repeated and if there is a possible error, stricter and more sagaciously controlled observation enables an ever increasing approach to a truth that is permanent, to a God who, while comprehending my reason, surpasses it, and whom my reason cannot deny.

A God without charity. But Yours has none either — none, that is, that you do not lend Him. Everything is inhuman — save man himself. We must make up our minds to it. And from that we must start. Yes, we must start.

I believe more easily in the Greek gods than in the 'Bon Dieu'. But I am obliged to acknowledge that this polytheism is purely poetical — equivalent to fundamental atheism. It was for his atheism that Spinoza was condemned. And yet he looked up to Christ with greater love, greater respect, greater piety even, than many Catholics — and those the most obedient — but a Christ without divinity.

The Christian hypothesis? Inadmissible.

Nevertheless it is not by materialist observations of fact that it can be shaken.

Are we to consider that God has failed because we have caught him out in one of his conjuring tricks?

Are we to rob him of his thunderbolts because we have discovered how lightning is produced?

'Too many stars, too many worlds,' thinks X . . ., who says to himself that perhaps he might believe if he found in the skies only just enough heavenly bodies to suspend the earth, to cause its gravitation, to heat and light it, and to set its poets dreaming. But he knows he cannot consider our globe the centre of the Universe, nor consequently, the Redemption either. So he says, 'Christ is nothing to me, if he is not central, if he is not all.'

And yet it must be one thing or the other – but I have never been able to make up my mind which I find it more impossible to believe – an infinite space peopled with an infinity of worlds or a world limited to so many stars and not one more, where, outside the space in which they gravitate, is to be found – what? A bourn at which my mind knocks; a void in which it cannot fly; an obstructive presence or a prohibitive absence – an absence at once of subject and object – a progressive absence or an absence beginning where? – an absence which is a slow diminishing of presence or a sudden and complete suppression of it?

No; none of all this. And in ancient days people wondered in the same way how and where the earth came to an end. Until at last the time came when they understood that it was round and that the beginning and end of its perfect circumference met at the same point.

I managed to do very well without any certainties as soon as I acquired this one – that the human mind can have none. Once this is granted, what is to be done? Are we to create them or accept pretences and endeavour not to think them false? – or learn to do without them? It was this that I set myself whole-heartedly to do. I refused to admit that such a relinquishment must drive man to despair.

BOOK III

It is towards pleasure that all nature's efforts tend. It is pleasure that makes the blade of grass grow, the bud develop, and the flower bloom. It is pleasure that opens the corolla to the sunbeam's kisses, invites every living thing to espousals, sends the obtuse larva to its nymphosis and from the prison of its chrysalis makes the butterfly escape. With pleasure for a guide, all things aspire to greater thriving, to increased consciousness, to progress. . . . And this is why I have found more instruction in pleasure than in books; why I have found in books more obfuscation than light.

There was no deliberation nor method about it. It was unreflectively that I plunged into this ocean of delights, astonished to find myself swimming in it, not to feel myself sinking. It is in pleasure that we become wholly conscious of ourselves.

All this took place of no set purpose; it was quite naturally that I let myself go. I had of course heard it said that human nature was bad, but I wanted to put it to the proof. I felt indeed less curious about myself than about others — or rather, the secret workings of carnal desire drove me out of myself towards an enchanting confusion.

To seek a system of morals did not seem to me very wise, nor even possible, as long as I did not know who and what I was. When I stopped looking for myself it was in love that I found myself again.

For some time I had to consent to the abandonment of all moral considerations and cease resisting my desires. They alone were capable of instructing me. I yielded to them.

'Oh!' said the poor invalid, 'if only for once . . . if only for once I could hold in my arms "whomsoever I burn for" as Virgil says ... After tasting that joy, I think I should resign myself more easily to knowing no others. I should resign myself more easily to dying.'

'Unhappy young man,' I answered, 'that joy once tasted, you would only long for it more than ever. However much of a poet you may be, imagination in such things torments less than memory.'

'Is that how you console me?' he asked.

And yet how often on the point of gathering a joy, I have suddenly turned away from it as might an ascetic.

It was not renunciation, but such a perfect knowledge of what that felicity would be, that no realization could have instructed me further, and nothing remained but to pass on, with the certainty that the preparation of a pleasure can only lead to it by deflowering it, and that the most exquisite delights are those that ravish our whole being by surprise. But at any rate I had succeeded in getting rid of all reticence and modesty, the reserves of decency, the hesitations of timidity — of all that makes pleasure fearful and predisposes the soul to remorse after the flagging of the flesh. All the blossoming, all the flowering I met on my way seemed merely the echo, the reflection of the springtime I carried within me. I burned with such intensity that I felt I could communicate my fervour to every other creature, as one gives a light from one's cigarette and it only glows the brighter. I shook away from me all that was ash. Love, unconfined, unsubdued, laughed in my eyes. Goodness, I thought, is only a radiation of happiness; and I gave my heart to all as the simple result of being happy.

Then, later . . . No, it was not diminishing desire, nor satiety, that I felt with the approach of age; but often, as I forecast the too rapid draining of pleasure by my greedy lips, possession seemed to me less precious than pursuit and more and more I came to prefer thirst itself to the quenching of it, the promise to the reality of pleasure, and to satisfaction the infinite enlargement of love.

ENCOUNTERS

I WENT to see him in a village in the Valais where he was supposed to be completing his convalescence, but where, in reality, he was making ready to die. He was so changed by illness that I hardly recognized him.

'Well, no,' he said, 'I'm not well – not at all. All my organs have been attacked, one after the other – liver, kidneys, spleen . . . As for my knee! Have a look at it, just for curiosity's sake.'

And half lifting the bed-clothes and bringing his wasted leg into view, he showed me a kind of enormous ball just at the joint. As he was perspiring profusely, his shirt clung to his body and accentuated his extreme thinness. I tried to smile so as to hide what I was feeling.

'In any case, you knew your recovery would take a long time,' I said. 'But you're comfortable here, aren't you? The air is good. The food . . .?'

'Excellent. And the saving thing is that my digestion is still good. In the last few days I have even gained weight. I have less fever. Oh, all things considered, I'm decidedly better.'

The appearance of a smile twisted his features and I understood that perhaps he had not lost all hope.

'Besides, spring is upon us,' I said quickly, turning my face to the window, for my eyes were full of tears I wanted to hide. 'You will soon be able to sit in the garden.'

'I go into it already for a few minutes every day after the mid-day meal. For it's only my dinner I get taken up to my room. I force myself to have lunch in the dining-room and so far I have missed only three days. Going upstairs again afterwards to the second floor is rather a business; but I take it easy; not more than four steps at a time and then a pause to get my breath. In all it takes me a good twenty minutes. But it gives me a little exercise; and I'm so glad afterwards to get back to bed. And then it leaves them time to do my room. But what I'm most afraid of is giving in. . . . You're looking at my books? . . . Yes, that's your *Nourritures Terrestres*. That little book never leaves me. You can't imagine the consolation and encouragement I get out of it.'

This touched me more than any compliment I have ever had; for I confess I was afraid my book could only find a welcome from the strong.

'Yes,' he went on, 'even in my state, when I am in the garden now that it is on the point of flowering, I want to say like Faust to the passing moment, " *Verweile doch! Du bist so schön!*" I feel then that everything is harmonious, suave. . . . What troubles me is that I myself am, as it were, a false note in the concert, a blot on the picture. I do so wish I could have been handsome.'

He stayed some time without saying any more, his eyes turned to the blue sky which was visible through the wide open window. Then in a lower voice, and almost timidly, 'I wish,' he said, 'you would send news of me to my parents. I'm at such a pass now that I'm afraid of writing to them – and above all of telling them the truth. Whenever my mother gets a letter from me, she answers at once that if I'm ill, it's for my good; that God vouchsafes me these sufferings for the sake of my salvation; that I ought to reflect on it in order to amend, and that not till then shall I deserve to get well. Then I invariably tell her I am better, so as to avoid these reflections – they make me feel blasphemous. Write to her – you.'

'It shall be done this very morning,' I said, taking his damp hand.

'Oh! don't squeeze so hard. You're hurting me.'

He was smiling.

II

For a long time our literature — and particualrly during the romantic period — praised, cultivated and propagated sadness; not the active, resolute sadness that makes men rush to glorious deeds, but a kind of flabbiness of soul, which was called melancholy, which gave a becoming pallor to the poet's brow and filled his eyes with yearning. There was a great deal of fashion and snobbery in it. Happiness seemed vulgar — the sign of foolish good health, and laughter was an ugly grimace. Unhappiness reserved to itself the privilege of spirituality — and so of profundity.

As for me, who have always preferred Bach and Mozart to Beethoven, I consider Musset's greatly vaunted line:
'Les plus désespérés sont les chants les plus beaux'
a blasphemy, and I will not admit that men should allow themselves to be struck down by adversity.

Yes, I know there is more determination about this than a yielding to nature. I know that Prometheus, bound on the Caucasus, suffered, and Christ was crucified, both of them for having loved men. I know that alone among the demi-gods, Hercules bears on his brow the stamp of care, for having triumphed over monsters and hydras — all the dreadful powers that were keeping mankind in subjection. I know that there are still — and perhaps will always be — dragons to vanquish . . . But in the renunciation of joy there is a confession of failure, a kind of abdication, of cowardice.

That it should have been only at the expense of others, only by settling himself ruthlessly on top of his fellows, that man has hitherto risen to a state of comfort — a state in which happiness is possible — this is what we ought no longer to admit. I will not admit either that the greater number should be compelled to resign on this earth the happiness that naturally springs out of harmony.

But what men have made of the promised land — the granted land — is enough to make the gods blush. The child that breaks his toy, the animal that lays waste its pasture and muddies its drinking water, the bird that fouls its nest, are no stupider. Oh, the squalid approach to our towns! Ugliness, discord, stench! I think of the gardens our city-belts might become with the help of a little understanding and love — all that is most luxuriant and delicate in the way of vegetation protected, and every slightest attempt on the part of one to interfere with the pleasure of all, repressed.

I think of what Leisure might be! The benediction of joy over the spirit's playtime! And work, work itself, redeemed, retrieved from its primeval curse!

What evolutionist would ever suppose the slightest connection between the caterpillar and the butterfly – if it were not known that they are in fact the same creature? Filiation appears impossible – and there is identity. If I had been a naturalist, I think it is upon this enigma that I should have concentrated all the energies and enquiries of my mind.

Had it been given to only a very few of us to witness this metamorphosis, it would perhaps seem more astonishing. But we cease to be surprised at a constant miracle.

And not only does the shape change, but the habits, the appetites . . .

Know thyself. *A maxim as pernicious as it is ugly. To observe oneself is to arrest one's development. The caterpillar that tried 'to know itself' would never become a butterfly.*

Yes, I feel throughout my diversity a constancy; I feel that what is diverse in me is still myself. *But for the very reason that I know and feel the existence of this constancy, why should I strive to obtain it? All through my life I have never sought to know myself; that is to say I have never sought myself. It seemed to me that such seeking, or rather, the success of such seeking brought with it a limitation and impoverishment of self, and that only rather poor and limited personalities succeeded in finding and understanding themselves; or, more truly, that this self-knowledge limited the self and its development; for such as one found oneself, so one remained, anxious henceforth to resemble oneself; and that it was better to persevere in safeguarding future possibilities — the perpetual and elusive process of becoming. I dislike inconsistency less than a kind of persistent consistency, less than the determination to be true to oneself, and than the fear of giving oneself away. I think moreover that such inconsequence is only apparent and that it responds to some more secret continuity. I think too that here, as always, we are deceived by words, for language imposes on us more logic than often exists in life; and that the most precious part of ourselves is that which remains unformulated.*

III

I have sometimes — I have often — out of spite, spoken more ill than I thought of other people and, out of cowardice, more good than I thought of many works, books or pictures, for fear of setting their authors against me. I have sometimes smiled at people I did not think at all funny, and pretended to think silly remarks witty. I have sometimes pretended to enjoy myself when I was being bored to death and couldn't bring myself to go away because I was asked to stay. I have too often allowed my reason to stop the impulse of my heart. And, on the other hand, when my heart was silent, I have too often spoken notwithstanding. I have sometimes done foolish things in order to meet with approval. And, on the other hand, I have not always had the courage to do the things I thought I ought to do because I knew they would meet with disapproval.

Regret for the 'temporis acti' is the vainest occupation of the old man. I tell myself so, and yet I give way to it. You encourage me because you think such regret of a kind to bring the soul gradually back to God. But you mistake the nature of my regrets, of my remorse. It is regret for the 'non acti' that torments me — for all that I might have done, that I ought to have done, in my youth, and was prevented from doing by your code of morals — a code in which I no longer believe, though I believed it right to submit to it at the time when it was most irksome to me, so that I gave my pride the satisfaction I refused my flesh. For it is at that age when soul and body are most ready for love, worthiest to love and be loved, when the power to embrace is strongest, curiosity at its keenest and most instructive, pleasure most precious — it is at that age too that soul and body find the greatest power of resistance to the solicitations of love.

What you called, what I too called 'temptations' — those are what I regret; and if today I repent, it is not for having yielded to some of them, but for having resisted so many others, which later on I pursued, when they were less enchanting and less profitable for my mind.

I repent of having cast a gloom over my youth, of having preferred the imaginary to the real, of having turned aside from life.

'Oh!' they will think, when they are on the point of quitting this life, 'all that we didn't do and that we might have done! All that we ought to have done and that yet we didn't do! Out of too careful considering, out of laziness, out of procrastination, because we said, "Pooh! there will always be time enough!" Because we failed to gather the irreplaceable everyday, the irrecoverable every moment. Because we put off the decision, the effort, the embrace . . .'

The passing hour has passed indeed.

'Oh,' they will think, 'you, my successor, be more sensible. Seize the moment.'

I settle myself in this point of space I am occupying at this exact moment of time. I will not admit that it is not crucial. I stretch out my arms to their full length. 'This is the South,' I say, 'this the North . . . I am effect, I shall be cause. A determining cause — an occasion which will never arise again. I am; but I will have a reason for being. I will know what I am living for.'

The fear of ridicule drives us to the worst kinds of cowardice. How many young men, greatly aspiring, have had their convictions pricked like bubbles by the single word Utopia, *and by the fear of passing for visionaries in the eyes of sensible people! As if every great progress of mankind's were not due to a realization of some part of Utopia! As if tomorrow's reality would not be made of yesterday's and today's Utopia — that is, if the future is not a mere repetition of the past — a thought calculated to take from me every joy I have in living. Yes, without the idea of possible progress, life is of no value to me; and I adopt as my own the words I give the Alissa of my* Porte Étroite: *'However blessed it may be, I cannot wish for a state without progress . . . and I should scorn any joy that was not* progressive.'

Very few monsters deserve to be feared as we fear them. Monsters engendered of fear — fear of the dark and fear of the light; fear of death and fear of life; fear of others and fear of oneself; fear of the devil and fear of God — you will eventually cease to impose on us. But we still live in the reign of bugbears. Who was it said that the fear of God was the beginning of Wisdom? Imprudent wisdom — real wisdom — you begin where fear ends, and you teach us life.

To bring confidence, ease and joy wherever possible, this very soon be-came a necessity to which my indispensable happiness laid claim – as though it was only out of other people's happiness that I could make my own, for the only happiness I knew was that which I felt in sympathy and as it were by procuration. And consequently everything of a nature to prevent that happiness seemed to me hateful – timidities, discourage-ments, misunderstandings, backbiting, self-complacent dwelling on imaginary misfortunes, vain pinings for the unreal, the divisions of parties, classes, nations or races – everything, in fact, that tends to make man an enemy of himself or others – the sowing of discords, oppressions, intimidations, refusals.

The squirrel does not crawl like the snake. The hare takes to flight while the tortoise and the hedgehog shrink into themselves. You will find this diversity among men too. Cease then from blaming what differs from yourself. A society of men will never be perfect unless it can make use of many different forms of activity, unless it favours the flowering of many different forms of happiness.

Corrupters, debilitators, wet blankets, retrogrades, tardigrades and scoffers became my personal enemies.

I detest everything that belittles man, everything that tends to make him less wise, less confident or less prompt. For I cannot grant that wisdom should always be accompanied by slowness and mistrust. And this indeed is why I believe that there is often more wisdom in the child than in the old man.

THEIR wisdom? . . . Oh! their wisdom! Don't let's make too much of it.

It consists in living as little as possible, distrusting everything, taking endless precautions.

There is always something stale in their advice, something stagnant.

They are like those mothers who drive their children silly with injunctions:

'Don't swing so hard, the cord'll break.'

'Don't stand under that tree, it's going to thunder.'

'Don't walk in the wet, you'll slip.'

'Don't sit on the grass, you'll dirty yourself.'

'At your age you ought to know better.'

'How many times shall I have to tell you . . . not to put your elbows on the table . . .?'

'The child's unbearable!'

Oh, madam, far less than you!

At once surprising and anxiously awaited, I liken joy to the great bowl of fresh milk we found at the rest-house one overpoweringly hot evening after a day's march through a parched country. We had not seen milk for weeks, for the district we were travelling through was a prey to sleepy-sickness and unsuitable for cattle. But all unawares, we had a few hours earlier reached a safe region where cattle-breeding was again possible, and if the grass had not been so tall, or if our mounts had enabled us to see over it, we might have caught sight here and there in the bush, of grazing flocks. And that evening, we had only looked forward as usual to quenching our thirst with tepid, suspicious looking water, which we should first have had to boil out of prudence, and which would still have tasted nauseous in spite of the wine or spirits that coloured it. With this we had had to content ourselves during the previous days. But that evening in the shadow of the hut, what was our delight at finding this bowl of milk which had been especially milked for us. A thin film of grey sand had tarnished its surface. Our cups tore this fragile coating and the milk seemed all the more candid, all the cooler for the heat of the long day. Notwithstanding its whiteness, we felt it was shade we were drinking, and rest, and comfort.

BOOK IV

I

I care only for what lives and breathes. In reality, it is to organize that my mind labours — to construct; but I can build nothing unless I begin by testing the materials I am to use. My mind will not admit accepted notions and principles, unless it has itself accepted them. I know moreover that the most sounding words are the hollowest. I distrust declaimers, orthodox thinkers, smooth-tongued preachers. I start by pricking their speeches and letting the gas out. I want to know how much vain-glory lies in your virtue, how much self-interest in your patriotism, how much lust and selfishness in your love. No! my Heavens are not darkened because I no longer take lanterns for stars; my determination is not weakened by refusing to be guided by shadows, by no longer loving anything but truth.

But this certainty — that men have not always been what they are now, allows me this hope — that they will not for ever remain so.

I too, no doubt, have smiled or laughed with Flaubert at the idol of Progress; but it was because Progress was represented as a despicable deity. The progress of commerce and industry, of the arts especially — what an absurdity! The progress of knowledge — yes, certainly. But what really matters to me is the progress of Mankind.

That men have not always been what they are now, that they have slowly made themselves — this, I think, is no longer disputable, in spite of mythologies. If our survey is limited to a few centuries, we recognize in the past men like those of today, and are astonished that they have remained the same since the days of the Pharaohs; but this is no longer true, if we cast our eyes back into the abyss of prehistoric ages. And if they have not always been what they are now, why should we think they will always remain so?

Man is in process of becoming.

But there are people who imagine and want to persuade me that mankind resembles that one of Dante's damned who, despairing because he is condemned to eternal immobility, exclaims, 'If I could take only one step forward every thousand years, I should already be on the way.'

This idea of progress has taken root in my mind. It is related now to all my other ideas, or has dominated them.

(Any classical period, by reason of a momentarily acquired equilibrium, may give the illusion of a perfectly accomplished man.) The thought that man's actual state must necessarily be surpassed, is transporting and is at the same time accompanied by a hatred of anything that may prevent that progress, which may be compared to the Christian's hatred of evil.

All this will be swept away — what deserves to go and also what does not. For how is the one to be separated from the other? You want to seek mankind's salvation by clinging to the past, and it is only by thrusting away the past, by thrusting into the past all that has ceased to be of use, that progress becomes possible. But you will not believe in progress. What has been, you say, is what will be. I choose to believe that what has been is what can never be again. Man will gradually free himself from what formerly protected him — from what henceforth enslaves him.

It is not only the world that must change but man. Where will he come from, this new man? Not from the outside. Comrade, you must discover him in yourself, and, as the native ore casts its dross and emerges pure metal, you must call up out of yourself this coming man. Obtain him from yourself. Have courage to become yourself. Do not let yourself off too easily. There are great possibilities in every being. Believe in your strength and youth. Keep saying to yourself, 'It lies with me.'

Nothing satisfactory is to be got from crossbreeding.

When I was young, my brain was full of mongrels, mules, camelopards.

The virtue of selection.

The first virtue – patience.
Nothing to do with simple waiting. More like obstinacy.

ENCOUNTERS

I

In Bourbonnais, I once knew a charming old maid
    Who had a cupboard full of old medicines –
    So full that there was hardly any room left in it at all;
    And as the old lady was then perfectly well,
    I made so bold as to say that perhaps it was not a very good plan
    To keep so many things that were not the slightest use to her.
    Then the old lady got very red in the face,
    And I thought she was going to cry.
    She took out the bottles and the boxes and the tubes one after the other.
    'This,' she said, 'rid me of colic, and this of quinsy;
    This ointment cured me of an abcess in the groin
    Which might very well – one never knows – come on again;
    And these pills were a great comfort to me
    At a time when I suffered a little from constipation.
    As for this object, it must, I think, have been an inhaler,
    But I fear it has almost completely ceased to work. . . .'
    Finally she confessed that once upon a time all these medicaments had cost her a great deal of money,
    And I understood that it was really this that prevented her from getting rid of them.

2

    Then the time comes when we must leave all this.
    What will this 'all this' be? For some people it will be
    Hoards of accumulated wealth, estates, libraries,
    Divans on which to enjoy pleasure,
    Or simply leisure;

For many others it will be toil and trouble;
To leave family and friends, children who are growing up;
Tasks begun, a work to accomplish,
A dream on the point of fulfilment;
Books they wanted to read;
Perfumes they had never breathed;
Unsatisfied curiosities;
Unfortunates who counted on their help;
The peace, the serenity they were hoping to attain —
And then suddenly 'les jeux sont faits; rien ne va plus.'
And one fine day, someone says: 'You know — Gontran.
I've just been to see him. It's all up with him.
He's been in a bad way for the last week.
He kept saying, "I feel, I feel I'm going."
There was still some hope, though. But now there's none.'
'What's the matter with him?'
'They think it's the ductless glands,
But his heart was in a bad state.
A kind of insulin poisoning, said the doctor.'
'That's a queer thing.'
'They say he's left a fairly large fortune,
A collection of coins and pictures.
His collaterals won't get a penny on account of the death-duties.'
'Coins! That's a thing I can't understand people being interested in.'

You needn't pretend to be so clever. You have seen people die; there's nothing very funny about it. You try to joke so as to hide your fear; but your voice trembles and your sham poem is frightful.

Perhaps . . . Yes, I have seen people die. In most cases it seemed to me that just before death and once the crisis was past, the sharpness of the sting was in a way blunted. Death puts on velvet gloves to take us. He does not strangle us without first lulling us to sleep, and the things he robs us of have already lost their distinctiveness, their presence and, as it were, their reality. The universe becomes so colourless that it is no longer very difficult to leave it, and nothing is left to regret.

So I say to myself that it can't be so difficult to die since, as a matter of fact, everybody manages it. And after all, it would perhaps be nothing but a habit to fall into, if only one died more than once.

But death is dreadful to those who have not filled their lives. In their case, it is only too easy for religion to say: 'Never mind! It's in the other world that things begin. You'll get your reward there.'

It is now *and in* this *world that we must live.*

Comrade, believe in nothing — accept nothing without proof. Never anything was proved by the blood of martyrs. No religion, however mad, that has not had its own, none that has failed to rouse passionate convictions. It is in the name of faith that men die; in the name of faith they they kill. The desire for knowledge springs from doubt. Stop believing and begin learning. It is only when proofs are lacking that people try to impose their opinions. Do not let yourself be credulous. Do not let yourself be imposed on.

Traumatism — deadens pain . . .

See Montaigne's admirable account of his fainting fit, after he had been thrown from his horse; and Rousseau's story of the accident which nearly cost him his life: 'I felt neither the blow nor the fall, nor anything that followed, until I came to myself again. . . . Night was approaching. I had a glimpse of the sky, a few stars and a little green. This first sensation was a delicious moment. As yet I was conscious of myself in that alone. In that instant I was born to life and felt as though I were filling every object I beheld with my own aerial existence. Entirely absorbed by the present moment, I remembered nothing. . . . I felt neither pain, nor fear, nor anxiety. . . .'

There was a little book on natural history which I lost at the beginning of the war and have been looking for ever since in vain. I remember neither its title nor the name of its author. (It was a small English book with illustrations and bound in dark red cloth.) I had read only the introduction, which was a sort of invitation to the study of so-called natural science. It said (and this I remember very well) that, speaking roughly, pain was a human invention, that in nature everything concurred to avoid it, and that it would be reduced to very little, except for man's intervention. Not that every living creature is not capable of suffering; but, in the first place, every sickly and deformed creature is, as it were, automatically suppressed. Some striking examples were then given; among others that of the hen which, after it has just escaped from the hawk's talons, immediately starts pecking its grain again, as free from care as ever. For, said the author, and I agree with him, animals live in the present, so that they are spared the greater number of our ills, most of which are imaginary, attached as they are to the recollection of the past (regrets, remorse) or to the apprehension of the future. The author, enlarging on his theory, with which, bold as it was, I at once concurred, maintained that the hare or the deer, when it is being pursued (not by man but by another animal), enjoys its flight, its leaps and feints. Finally, there is this which we know to be true: the blow of the wild beast's paw, like all violent traumatisms, stuns, so that for the most part the prey succumbs without feeling any pain. I see of course that this theory, if pushed too far, might appear paradoxical, but I believe it on the whole to be perfectly true, and that the happiness of existence greatly outweighs its suffering throughout nature, until we get to man. But that it ceases to be true in his case — and by his own fault.

If he were not so insane, he might spare himself the ills caused by war, and if he were less ferocious towards his fellows those caused by poverty, which are by far the most numerous. This is no Utopia, but the simple recognition of the fact that most of our ills have nothing inevitable or necessary about them and are due only to ourselves. As for those we cannot avoid, if there are diseases, there are also remedies. Nothing will prevent me from thinking that humanity might be more vigorous than it is, healthier and consequently happier, and that we are responsible for almost all the ills from which we suffer.

If then I call nature God, it is for simplicity's sake and because it irritates the theologians. For you may have noticed that such people shut their eyes to nature, or if they happen to glance at it, they are incapable of observing it.

Instead of trying to get instruction from men, let your teaching come from God. Man has grown crooked. His history is simply that of his false pretences and his sham excuses. 'A market-gardener's cart,' I once wrote, 'carries with it more truths than Cicero's finest periods.' There is man's history and the history so rightly called natural. *In* Natural History *you must listen to the voice of God. And don't be satisfied with listening to it vaguely; put definite questions to God and insist on his answering you definitely. Don't be satisfied with gazing — observe.*

You will notice then that everything that is young is tender. In how many sheathes is not every bud wrapped round! But all that at first protected the tender germ, when once germination is accomplished, hinders it; and no growth is possible unless it bursts the sheathes in which at first it was swaddled.

Mankind clings to its swaddling-clothes, but it will never grow unless it succeeds in getting rid of them. The child that has been weaned is not ungrateful if it pushes away its mother's breast. It is no longer milk that it needs. Comrade, you must refuse henceforth to seek your nourishment in the milk of tradition, man-distilled and man-filtered. You have teeth now with which to bite and chew and you must find your food in what is real. Stand up erect, naked and valiant; burst your wrappings, push aside your props; to grow straight you need nothing now but the urge of your sap and the sun's call.

You will notice that every plant casts its seeds to a distance; either the seeds have a delicious covering that tempts the bird's appetite, so that they are carried to places they could not otherwise reach; or else, equipped with spirals or feathers, they trust themselves to the wandering breezes. For, if it nourishes the same kind of plant too long, the soil becomes impoverished and poisonous, and the new generation cannot find its food in the same place as the preceding one. Do not try to eat again what your fathers before you have already digested. Look at the winged seeds of the plane or the sycamore flying off as if they understood that the paternal shade can offer them nothing but a dwindling and atrophied existence.

And you will notice too that the rush of the sap goes preferably to swell the buds at the extreme tips of the branches, those that are furthest from the trunk. Understand this rightly and put the longest possible distance between you and the past.

Understand rightly the Greek fable. It teaches us that Achilles was invulnerable except in that spot of his body which had been made soft by the remembrance of his mother's touch.

You shall not get the better of me, sadness! Through lamentations and sobs, I can hear the sweet sounds of singing. The words are my own invention and they bring courage to my heart when it begins to fail me. I fill that song with your name, comrade, and with an appeal to those undaunted hearts who will answer it.

Up! Up then, bowed heads! Look up, eyes bent down towards the grave! Look up! Not to the empty heavens, but to the earth's horizon! Wherever your steps lead you, comrade, let your hope bear you on, regenerate, valiant, ready to quit these spots befouled with the stench of the dead. Let no love of the past hold you back. Hasten forward to the future. No longer transfer your poetry to your dreams; learn to see it in reality. And, if as yet you cannot — put it there.

Unquenched thirsts, unsatisfied appetites, fevers, vain longings, fatigues, insomnia — all this, comrade, oh! how I wish it may be spared you! How I wish I could bend within reach of your hands, of your lips, the branches of all fruit-trees. Raze all walls; bring down before you all barriers on which a jealous ownership has written 'No admittance. Private property.' Obtain at last that the reward of your toil may come to you in its entirety. That your heads may be raised, and your hearts allowed at last to be filled, not with hate and envy, but with love. Yes! That all the sweetness of the air, all the rays of the sun and all the invitations of happiness may be at last allowed to reach you.

Passionately leaning over the vessel's prow, I watch, advancing towards
me, the innumerable waves, the islands, the adventures of the unknown
land which already . . .

'No,' *he said,* 'your image is wrong. You can see the waves, you can
see the islands; but the future we cannot see — only the present. I see
what the moment brings; think you of what it takes away and of what I
shall never see again. A man standing at the vessel's prow sees nothing
in front of him, metaphorically speaking, but an immense void.* . . .'

'Which is filled with possibilities. What has been matters less to me
than what is; what is less than what may be and will be. To my mind
the possible and the future are one. I believe that all that is possible is
striving to come into being; that all that can be will be, if man helps.'

'And you say you are not a mystic! But yet you know well enough
that of these possibilities, one only, in order to come into being, must
thrust all the others back into non-being, and that what might have
been can move us to nothing but regret.'

'I know best of all that one can only go forward by pushing the past
behind one. We are told that Lot's wife, because she looked behind her,
was changed into a pillar of salt — that is, of frozen tears. Turning towards the future, Lot then lies with his daughters. So be it!'

O you for whom I write — whom in other days I called by a name which seems to me now too plaintive — Nathaniel — whom today I call comrade — rid your heart henceforth of all that is plaintive.

Obtain from yourself all that makes complaining useless. No longer implore from others what you yourself can obtain.

I have lived. It is your turn now. It is in you that my youth will be prolonged. I pass you my powers. If I feel that you are my successor, I shall resign myself more easily to dying. I hand on my hopes to you.

The knowledge that you are brave and strong enables me to leave life without regret. Take my joy. Let your happiness be to increase that of others. Work and strive and accept no evil that you might change. Keep saying to yourself, 'It lies with me.' One cannot resign oneself to the evils that come from men without baseness. Cease believing, if you ever believed it, that wisdom consists in resignation; or else cease laying claim to wisdom.

Comrade, do not accept the life that is offered you by men. Never cease to be convinced that life might be better — your own and others'; not a future life that might console us for the present one and help us to accept its misery, but this one of ours. Do not accept. As soon as you begin to understand that it is not God but man who is responsible for nearly all the ills of life, from that moment you will no longer resign yourself to bearing them.

Do not sacrifice to idols.

END

MORE ABOUT PENGUINS
AND PELICANS

Penguinews, which appears every month, contains details of all the new books issued by Penguins as they are published. From time to time it is supplemented by *Penguins in Print,* which is our complete list of almost 5,000 titles.

A specimen copy of *Penguinews* will be sent to you free on request. Please write to Dept EP, Penguin Books Ltd, Harmondsworth, Middlesex, for your copy.

In the U.S.A.: For a complete list of books available from Penguin in the United States write to Dept CS, Penguin Books Inc., 7110 Ambassador Road, Baltimore, Maryland 21207.

In Canada: For a complete list of books available from Penguin in Canada write to Penguin Books Canada Ltd, 41 Steelcase Road West, Markham, Ontario.

THE IMMORALIST

André Gide

This is the story of a man's rebellion against social and sexual conformity. The narrator is Michel – a rich, young, agnostic scholar who has just married and gone to stay with his wife in Algeria. Finding that he has tuberculosis, he gradually changes his life, abandoning the aspects of morality which restrict him, and following his own wants and needs.

This development is the author's theme, but it does not obscure the other characters in the novel: Michel's wife Marceline, various members of Parisian society, the youths on his estate in the country, and Arab boys.

The problems which are posed in *The Immoralist* are ones which exercised Gide himself in his own life – how deep is the protective veneer of civilization, and to what extent should a man follow his own desires when they conflict with society?

Also available

THE COUNTERFEITERS

JOURNALS 1889–1949

STRAIT IS THE GATE

LA SYMPHONIE PASTORALE *and* ISABELLE

THE VATICAN CELLARS